There was no easy way out.

Telling him about the pregnancy would clearly lead to him knowing about Emmylou Brown, and that would lead to absolute heartbreak.

But not telling him just wasn't right.

That's how she found herself in the San Antonio parking structure of his office building.

Emmy knew he'd be here.... The question was, would she get out of the car when he arrived?

He emerged from the elevator.

Do it now, she thought, forcing herself to step outside to intercept him.

"Deston."

Dear Reader,

Spring might be just around the corner, but it's not too late to curl up by the fire with this month's lineup of six heartwarming stories. Start off with *Three Down the Aisle*, the first book in bestselling author Sherryl Woods's new miniseries, THE ROSE COTTAGE SISTERS. When a woman returns to her childhood haven, the last thing she expects is to fall in love! And make sure to come back in April for the next book in this delightful new series.

Will a sexy single dad find *All He Ever Wanted* in a search-and-rescue worker who saves his son? Find out in Allison Leigh's latest book in our MONTANA MAVERICKS: GOLD RUSH GROOMS miniseries. The Fortunes of Texas are back, and you can read the first three stories in the brand-new miniseries THE FORTUNES OF TEXAS: REUNION, only in Silhouette Special Edition. The continuity launches with *Her Good Fortune* by Marie Ferrarella. Can a straitlaced CEO make it work with a feisty country girl who's taken the big city by storm? Next, don't miss the latest book in Susan Mallery's DESERT ROGUES ongoing miniseries, *The Sheik & the Bride Who Said No*. When two former lovers reunite, passion flares again. But can they forgive each other for past mistakes? Be sure to read the next book in Judy Duarte's miniseries, BAYSIDE BACHELORS. A fireman discovers his ex-lover's child is *Their Secret Son*, but can they be a family once again? And pick up Crystal Green's *The Millionaire's Secret Baby*. When a ranch chef lands her childhood crush—and tycoon—can she keep her identity hidden, or will he discover her secrets?

Enjoy, and be sure to come back next month for six compelling new novels, from Silhouette Special Edition.

All the best,

Gail Chasan
Senior Editor

Please address questions and book requests to:
Silhouette Reader Service
U.S.: 3010 Walden Ave., P.O. Box 1325, Buffalo, NY 14269
Canadian: P.O. Box 609, Fort Erie, Ont. L2A 5X3

The Millionaire's Secret Baby

CRYSTAL GREEN

Silhouette

SPECIAL EDITION

Published by Silhouette Books

America's Publisher of Contemporary Romance

To the energetic, enthusiastic, and consistently inspirational
people of www.eHarlequin.com! From the Daily Online
Serial to the Teahouse to the Bat Cave to the Hollywood
Boards: You all give me a great reason to write. Special
thanks to Beverly "Gazpacho" for Emmy's Scalloped
Tomatoes with Pearl Onions recipe. There will be
many happy tummies because of you!

 SILHOUETTE BOOKS

ISBN 0-373-24668-4

THE MILLIONAIRE'S SECRET BABY

Printed in U.S.A.

Books by Crystal Green

Silhouette Special Edition

Beloved Bachelor Dad #1374
*The Pregnant Bride #1440
*His Arch Enemy's Daughter #1455
*The Stranger She Married #1498
*There Goes the Bride #1522
Her Montana Millionaire #1574
*The Black Sheep Heir #1587
The Millionaire's Secret Baby #1668

*Kane's Crossing

CRYSTAL GREEN

lives in San Diego, California, where she writes for Silhouette Special Edition, Silhouette Bombshell and Harlequin Blaze. When she isn't penning romances, she loves to read, overanalyze movies, pet her parents' Maltese dog, fence, do yoga and fantasize about being a really good cook.

Whenever possible, Crystal loves to travel. Her favorite souvenirs include journals—the pages reflecting everything from taking tea in London's Leicester Square to wandering the neon-lit streets of Tokyo.

She'd love to hear from her readers at: 8895 Towne Centre Drive, Suite 105-178, San Diego, CA 92122-5542.

And don't forget to visit her Web site at http://www.crystal-green.com!

SCALLOPED TOMATOES
WITH PEARL ONIONS

4 tbsp butter
*10 oz can pearl onions (may substitute 10 oz of leeks
cut in coins)*
1 clove garlic, minced
1 dozen fresh mushrooms, sliced
3 tbsp flour
28 oz can good quality Roma tomatoes
1 tbsp sugar
1/4 cup shredded fresh basil
salt and freshly ground pepper
Cubed bread or crumbs
Grated Parmesan cheese

Melt butter in a large heavy-bottomed pan. Add onions, garlic and mushrooms and sauté lightly. You can also add stir-fried veggies to this.

Sprinkle flour over onions (and veggies) and stir gently until well incorporated. Cook while stirring for a couple of minutes. Stir in tomatoes with their juices, then the sugar. Stir and bring just to a simmer. Stir in basil, then salt and pepper to taste.

Turn into a casserole dish, top with buttered bread cubes and Parmesan cheese. (If you don't have prepared bread cubes, tear up 4-6 slices of bread, lightly fry in butter, coat with garlic powder and Parmesan.)

Bake at 350°F until bubbly and bread is browned—approximately 30 minutes. Serves 6-8.

Chapter One

"**Y**ou're going to get burned, darlin'."

At first, Emmylou Brown thought the voice—a rough drawl scratching along the low, smooth edges of Texas Hill Country—was just part of the blank sleep she'd drifted into.

Disoriented, she opened her eyes and stared at the endless blue sky. The limestone ridge overlooking the swimming hole abraded her bare back, and her head swam from the heat of the sun.

The voice continued, tinged with wry amusement. "You might want to turn over. The weather's got some scorch to it."

Okay, this was no figment of her imagination.

She settled herself up on her elbows, glanced in the direction of the voice. Caught her breath.

The man sat on top of a chestnut quarterhorse, forearm propped on his saddle horn as he inspected her lazily. Scuffed boots with the heels hinged in stirrups, faded jeans stretching the length of his legs, a denim shirt covering wide shoulders and a powerful chest, a Stetson tipped over his cocked brow. Pure cowboy.

Except Emmy knew better.

She gulped, unable to say a word, a ridiculous attraction from years past freezing her in place.

Deston Rhodes.

Did he know who she was, even though they hadn't been on the ranch at the same time in twelve years?

Her stomach somersaulted, scrambling itself into a mishmash of jubilation. His attention warmed her through and through. She'd fantasized about him since childhood: Deston, sweeping her into his arms like she was a blessed princess, him murmuring, "I always did have my eye on you, Emmylou."

But as he grinned at her, she realized what he must really be seeing.

A pint-sized twenty-four-year-old waif in frayed jean shorts, the ones she'd torn the legs off of when they'd become too holey to wear in public. A girl wearing a too-tight, worn hankie top purchased from a last-chance sale in a San Antonio mall seven years ago—before she'd left Wycliffe, Texas, to expand her culinary horizons.

She sat up, crossing her arms over her clothes. But she couldn't hold back a vulnerably hopeful smile. The boss's son had finally taken note of her, had finally seen past her dull sheen of poverty. Hallelujah!

It was almost too much to wish for.

His horse shifted, and Deston moved with the disruption, his thigh muscles flexing as he controlled the animal without much effort.

"They told me you were somewhere on the property, and it'd be polite to reintroduce myself," he said. "I'm Deston. The grown-up version, that is."

So he *did* recognize her.

He waited, obviously expecting her to return the greeting.

But she was still tongue-tied. *The* Deston Rhodes was talking to Emmy as if they'd been pals, as if she wasn't the daughter of the late Nigel Brown, Mr. Rhodes's personal butler, or as if she wasn't the girl who'd take over for her mother, Francesca, in the kitchens someday.

Odd. Life on Oakvale Ranch usually didn't work this way. The upstairs people didn't consort with the ones downstairs, especially if they were the daughter of a man who had lost his family's nest egg in bad investments. A good man who'd left a wife and child to keep on struggling in debt, even after his death.

Oh, my.

Deston's gaze was coasting over her body, and the hairs on Emmy's limbs tingled with the thrill of it.

Was he checking her out?

She needed to act as if this were an everyday occurrence.

Coolly tilting her head toward the sun, she said, "It's good to see you again, Deston."

"Likewise." He paused, burning her with his direct stare, his topsy-turvy charm. "You know, I'm trying to think of why I ever called you Lemon Face."

Emmy's wishful thinking burst. He'd had a secret nickname for her and it was... "Lemon Face?"

"Don't look so thunderstruck. Don't you remember? I used to tease you about, well, everything, and you'd make this awful expression. Like you were sucking on lemons."

Wait. Deston had never teased Emmylou Brown. Ever.

They'd never even exchanged a word. She'd been just one of many servants' children, and he'd been a future millionaire in the making. Heck, she'd never even made eye contact with him, afraid of what she'd find embedded in his gaze: derision, distance, emptiness.

All the hope, all the happiness of finally being acknowledged by her childhood crush abandoned her in one big sigh.

He thought she was someone else. Some lucky socially-equal playmate from days gone by.

Of course, that's it. You're nothing but a convenience to all the Rhodes family. They don't even know you exist except for your cooking.

But she knew better. She could be so much more than that. Someday.

Emmy closed her eyes, blocking him out. For a second there she'd preened under his girl-you-grew-up-good gaze. She'd been someone who mattered to him.

Well, it was time to set him straight, to go back to reality. She prepared to tell him who she was, to watch as disinterest stiffened his spine to a more Rhodes-like posture of entitlement. Wasn't it unfortunate that she couldn't be his old friend, the woman who'd caught his eye? A person who'd probably never had to hide hole-gouged sneakers under a school desk in utter shame. A girl who'd probably never had a teacher try to slip her lunch money because she'd "forgotten" it three days in a row—when, actually, Emmy had stuffed the dollars her mama had given her back into her parents' stash, knowing it'd do more help there than in her stomach.

Even now she appreciated the irony. A cook's daughter, going without a meal.

When she opened her eyes again, he was still watching her, and Emmy almost melted all over the rock.

"Damn," he said. "You went and got prettier on me. You're sure not the Lemon Face I recall."

She sure wasn't.

With a this-could-have-been-so-beautiful grin, she turned over on the rock, away from him, resting her chin on her fist. "I'm *not* the girl you think I am."

She heard him chuckle, slide off his mount, rustle around as he secured the horse to a tree. "All right. So maybe you've grown out of the nickname. Hell, a lot of things have changed since we were kids."

Well, that hadn't worked. She was talking literally, and he wasn't.

His boots crunched over the fallen oak leaves, the birds cutting off their warbling as he passed them. "My parents said you're leaving the ranch today. I'm sorry I haven't been to many dinners in the big house or barbecues on the back lawn. Business swallowed me right up. But you understand, I'm sure, being a Stanhope."

Stanhope? The name sounded vaguely familiar, probably because it denoted one of a thousand guests who'd stayed at the ranch. Emmy spared him a glance from her prone position, her heart clenching.

The man of her youthful dreams, framed by a thicket of juniper and a passel of butterflies dancing around a tuft of hackberry. A knotted rope that the servant kids had used long ago to swing into the spring-fed pond dangled in front of him, and he reached out for it, fisting the hemp. The tendons in his forearm strained, leading up to the bunched muscles disappearing beneath his rolled-up sleeves. With the other hand, he whipped off his Stetson, revealing brown hair, green eyes. A football-hero grin.

"At least you recognized the old swimming hole," he said.

Would he be standing here, shooting the breeze, *flirting,* by gosh, if he knew she was below him?

No. The senior Mr. Rhodes would never stand for it. And neither would her self-confidence, actually.

But this was a moment she'd always fantasized about. Could she get away with just talking with him, living a dream for a harmless few minutes?

She swallowed. What the heck. She'd never get this chance again.

"I thought this place might offer some peace and quiet." Was that her with the siren voice? It was so easy to be someone other than Emmy. "But then you appeared."

Deston pretended to stumble back, hand over his heart. "Hey, if I'm infringing on your good time, I'll get going. But at least I got you to turn over before your front was fried to a crisp."

"I'm much obliged." See, this was no big deal, having a normal conversation with a demigod.

"Don't mention it." He stepped out of the shade, into the sunlight, nearer to her. "Anything else I can do?"

"You can fetch my water." What a fun turnabout. A *Rhodes* serving *her.* This had to be the first sign of the world's demise.

He shrugged, came closer, grabbed the bottle and held it out.

Emmy hitched in a breath. She'd never seen him this close before. Sure, she and her friends—other kids whose parents served on the ranch—had peeked through bushes at the Rhodes boys: Harry, with his untamable cowlick, Deston, with his shirttail always trailing out of his pants until Mrs. Rhodes would tuck it back in and shake her head at his carelessness. The girls would giggle to each other, every one taking a turn at imagining ways that Harry or Deston would propose to them.

In a jet to Monte Carlo? On a ballroom floor? On a yacht?

They'd played their hide-and-sigh games until Harry and Deston had each gone off to prep school. Then college. Mama had told Emmy that Deston had come back to San Antonio a few years ago to become a businessman just like his father.

But, by then, Emmy had gone off to complete her own destiny, reluctantly using the gift of her parents' life savings in order to train for the job she'd always been expected to assume.

But now, Deston was right here, so close she could lift her hand and touch the long spiky strands of his hair. So close she could smell a hint of sage on his tanned skin, see it in the green of his eyes. There was a slight dimple in his strong chin, too, and a touch of stubble slinking along his jawline.

"Thanks," she ribbeted, doing her best impression of a toad. Grabbing the water, she fiddled with the top, hating that he made her feel as if she was always craning her neck to catch sight of him. A boy on a pedestal.

Now a man.

Oh, yeah. All man.

He crouched next to her, setting his Stetson on the limestone, waiting.

What should she do? Emmy wasn't exactly a world-class flirt, especially after what had happened in Italy…. Not that it mattered now. Nope. It was just that she'd heard about all Deston's brief romances from the servants, who'd caught her up on every detail the minute she'd walked through the downstairs door.

Talk to him, she thought. Chat, just chat.

"So," she said, buying time. How did his friend act? Did he even know, not having seen her for years, either?

He grinned, his gaze brushing over Emmy's short, layered hair, over the curve of her back. Goose pimples winged over her skin.

"I've kept up on your life," she said. Good, that much was true. She'd stick to basic gossip, keeping the situation as innocuous as possible. "You were such a football star in school. Quarterback, right?"

He lifted up a hand in resignation, glanced away. "That's over and done with."

"Why didn't you keep at it? You were supposed to be pretty good." He'd been the best. She knew because she and her friends, Carlota and Felicia, had faithfully followed the papers, the gossip.

"I always knew I was meant to run Rhodes Industries one day," Deston said. He grabbed a twig from the ground, bent it, straightened it. "But my family gets a lot of mileage out of the whole Longhorn quarterback mystique."

"It does add prestige to your business image, doesn't it?"

He snapped the twig, tossed it away. Stood to his full height. His body cast a shadow over Emmy, all harnessed strength and dark memory.

"Isn't that why your father wanted to spend time here on the ranch?" he asked. "Because he wanted to talk statistics and relive a few glorified touchdowns?"

Her Papa? Nigel Brown, bless him, was thirteen years gone. And he'd be miffed by his daughter wanting to be anyone other than what she was born for.

She opened her mouth to correct Deston's assumptions, but he was talking again.

"That's how Edward Rhodes the Third draws them in, with promises of pigskin glamour and riches beyond imagination."

A threat of bitterness laced his words. She knew about Mr. Rhodes, how strict he was about running the ranch, the staff, the polished reputation of a millionaire family.

She couldn't see Deston's face, thanks to the sun's angle. Good thing, because once she revealed she wasn't from the Stanhope family, she didn't want to see his reaction.

There was a loud thrashing from across the swimming hole, and they both glanced over to see what had caused the racket.

A white-tailed deer had emerged from the foliage, gracefully walking along the water's edge.

"Look," Emmy said, momentarily lost in the sight. It'd been a long time since she'd been in Hill Country, and she'd missed it terribly.

The animal sensed them, stiffened, then burst away in a flash of legs and brown hide.

Deston leaned down, casually plucked at the knot that held together the back of Emmy's hankie top, then stood again. "Come on, let's make the most of your last day here, Lila."

He started to unbutton his shirt.

Lila. "Hey, I—" Her mouth clamped shut.

He'd whipped off the material, revealing tanned skin, work-honed muscles, abs that you could grate cheese on. When he undid the fly of his jeans, Emmy averted her eyes.

"I need to tell you something."

"What?" Heavy denim thumped in front of her, bodiless.

Oh, mercy. He was—as her mama might say— *nudo,* wasn't he?

Unable to help herself, Emmy peeked out of the corner of her gaze. She caught a glimpse of white boxers. Phew. Or maybe not. No, definitely phew. The last thing she needed was to be out in the middle of the boonies with a buck-naked boss's son. She'd get Mama fired in a second flat after what had happened a few years ago between Harry Rhodes and the maid, and, Lord knew, Mama needed every penny....

"You just gonna sit there?" Deston asked.

Emmy nodded, staring straight ahead. Should she concentrate on her book now? *Like Water for Chocolate,* something she'd read and used for recipes a million times before.

"Suit yourself." He whisked by her, body arching into the pond like a switchblade cocked open.

Deston obviously knew the depths of the swimming hole from his youth. When the servant kids had played here, they'd vacated the hole at the first sign of a Rhodes.

Emmy had never seen him swim, never seen him knife upward in a spray of droplets. The water sprinkled onto her arms, and she leaned backward.

"Hey!"

He laughed, clearly having the time of his life, slinging the hair out of his eyes with one whip of his head, pushing into a backstroke as he aimed another burst of water at her.

"Come in," he yelled, turning over and swimming away.

Moisture sluiced off the sinew of his back, trickling over the smooth taper of muscle flowing into waist. His boxers were plastered to the rounds of his backside, hugging the indentation right below his hips. She could imagine fitting her palm there, tracing the ridges of him.

Emmy watched him move effortlessly, athletically, parting the water before him. Diving beneath the surface, he disappeared.

She inhaled, spellbound, while fingering a fringe on her old, ugly shorts.

He'd asked her to come in. With him. *Her.* Emmylou Brown, a girl who was no more important than a piece of furniture in the Rhodes sitting room.

But what if she could be more than that?

Years ago, with Paolo, she'd asked the same question, and the answer had cut the heart right out of her.

This time though, what if she really could pretend she wasn't poor-girl Emmy? What if she could convince Deston she was an equal before he could guess who she really was?

Emmy bit her lip. And what if she could do it by being Lila Stanhope, even for an hour?

She crept closer to the edge of the stone slab, wondering if she'd be brave enough to dive in.

Underwater. Peace.

That's all Deston wanted. The silence you could hear below the pond's surface, where nothing existed but the present, the sunlight waving through the water.

He held his breath, lungs near to bursting, then with a thrust of energy, surged upward, breaking toward the sky.

The first thing he saw was Lila, one of his father's ranch guests. He faintly remembered her as a kid, but something had happened on the trip from the blurry Lemon Face of his recollection to today's woman. Now, she had a smile that lit up from the inside, brightening her dark cocoa eyes, her dusky skin. Even her hair was a point of light, short, shaped into bouncy layers. It looked like ginger to him. Ginger with vanilla streaks flowing over the strands near her face.

Damn, he hadn't remembered Lila Stanhope being such a beaut, just a girl with stringy brown hair and a nondescript stare. If he'd known that she'd turn out so gorgeous, he might have agreed right off the bat to what his father had been nagging him to do for a week now.

If you act sweet on her, Mr. Rhodes had said in his lecture voice, *business with the Stanhopes will go much smoother.*

Deston was a sight too old for lectures. At the age of twenty-nine, he was ready to think for himself. Had been for years. And he'd come to the conclusion—all on his own, if that could be believed—that courting Lila Stanhope in the name of corporate interests was not his style.

His father's eye had once again turned to the Stanhopes. That's why Deston hadn't seen Lila lately. Because Mr. Rhodes had lost interest in Stanhope Steel.

Until now.

Deston would do anything for his family. Work long hours, forgo a personal life in the process. Anything, except go against his own instincts.

Instincts. Bothersome jabs of fear that had everything to do with Juliet Templeton—the woman he'd loved and lost so tragically—and nothing to do with logic. His "instincts" kept him sane, and they were telling him to steer clear of Lila Stanhope.

She was perched on the stone slab, hovering above the water, looking as high-strung as that deer they'd seen flit through here.

Instincts. But why couldn't he just enjoy her smile for the time being?

"What are you waiting for?" he asked.

She answered with one of those sunburst flashes. He'd never seen a person light up that way, especially the socialites he was normally with.

"You can swim, right?" He glided nearer to her.

"I don't know if I want to get my hair wet."

"Priss."

"Excuse me?"

Now he'd done it. She settled her petite body onto the rock's edge, sent him a dignified glance. In spite of her clothes, retro hippie wear, he decided, she carried herself as if she was wearing silk and diamonds.

"I get it," he said, treading water. "You're going to punish me."

"By…?"

"By judging me from on top of your mountain. Cut a guy a break. I came out here to get away from wheeling and dealing."

"I see. You just wanted to clear your brain." She

tilted her head, and something lethal kurplunked into his gut.

"I'm not cooperating very well, am I?" she asked.

He ignored his common sense, moved closer, to just below the rock. "I promise I won't splash you anymore."

She swung her shapely legs, leaning forward to see him, small, firm breasts pressed against the near see-through material of her summer top. If he looked hard enough, he could see the faint darkness of her nipples, the way they beaded against the cotton. He yearned for just a touch of them.

Grasping her slim ankle, he commanded, "Breathe."

She'd reared backward, eyes widening. "Don't you d—"

Too late. He gently tugged, bringing her into the water, catching her before she went all the way under, holding her body flush against his.

Neither of them moved, not for a long moment. It was as if she wasn't wearing a stitch of clothing—the cotton puckered to her breasts, outlining every curve as well as the hardened buds in the center of them. Beads of moisture trickled from her collarbone onto his thumbs.

The contact warmed his blood. It'd been so long since he'd held a woman like this—so innocently, but with a flame of expectation licking the surface of his skin. Something untouched, deeply hidden, stirred in-

side, competing with the hunger, wanting to be fulfilled, too.

Hell, no. Juliet had killed that part of him when
she'd died. She'd turned out to be someone he hadn't
known at all, and the betrayal had altered him forever.

In order to sweep that yearning back into its dark
place, he purposely allowed Lila to slide down the
length of his body, slowly, water making their skin
slick, heated.

There. Lust, pure and simple. Uncomplicated by
emotions.

One of her legs tentatively wrapped around him as
they came face to face, those breasts rubbing against
his upper chest, tearing him apart from the inside out
as that unnamable *something* refused to die. God, he
didn't want to face it again.

Both of them were breathing raggedly as he hesitated. He was an experienced guy, at least as far as sex
was concerned. He knew what came next. So why
wasn't he doing it?

Another moment passed, filled with the song of
birds, the flutter of a dragonfly's wings as it beat past
them, the smell of juniper, grass and…her. A mixture
of cinnamon, sweet spices.

This was wrong to lead her on when he couldn't
promise anything more than an afternoon of canoodling.
He had too much work to worry about and, in one week,
he'd even be relocating to New York to oversee business
there.

Lila Stanhope seemed too nice for that kind of love-'em-and-leave-'em charade. Too innocent to deal with his demons. She was the daughter of a corporate associate. A business deal. A commitment.

He loosened his hold on her, but his hunger for more tenderness didn't abate. It merely rested. Waited.

She paused, as if mortified by his silent retreat. Then she braced against his chest, lightly pushing away, creating further distance between them with a deft backstroke.

"That was mighty assertive of you," she said.

He liked her sense of humor. From the moment she'd told him to fetch her water bottle, he'd been drawn to her spirit. "It runs in the family."

"Right. The Rhodes clan. Vicious oil tycoons. Claw-wielding corporate devils."

"Not straight out of the gate. Edward the First, Great-great-great Granddad, was quite the gentleman."

"Do tell." She'd backed against a limestone cliff face to hold her up. The wet ends of her hair left dark trails near the snail fossils etched into the surface.

"You want a history lesson?" he asked, relieved by the possibility of small talk.

She raised her eyebrow and nodded. He'd bet that she was doing everything possible to cool the tension between them. But he couldn't forget the feel of her leg clenching him against her, the sight of her breasts.

Might as well humor her before she went running

to daddy about the big bad wolf in the woods, just like she used to.

"All right then. Edward the First was a third son of a duke, so of course he had no hope over in grand ol' England. He ended up over here in Texas, right before the War Between the States, and managed to finagle some land. He did a pretty decent job of raising cattle. But when the Great Depression rolled around and William Rhodes had the honor of taking over the family business, they had to entertain 'dudes' to keep the ranch solvent. We got rid of the city folk about fifty years ago though. No more need for them."

"Aren't we high and mighty?" She was too damned cute with her brow arched like that.

"Why're you offended? I'll bet you could outclass any dude by being able to distinguish one end of a horse from the other. Or maybe you just have a yen for hay rides and sing-alongs."

"My sentimental side does cry out for a good square dance every so often, I have to admit." She paused. "So your fortune wasn't made off dudes."

He'd sidestroked away from her. "Right. Back in the day, we invested in land north of here, and we struck oil. Millions were made, and that's when the family started acquiring businesses."

"And more businesses. And…"

They both laughed knowingly, and he shook his head. "If I'd known you were so sociable, I'd have straightaway locked my office up tight and hurried back to Wycliffe to meet you again."

"Yeah, sure," she said. "You've got the markings of a workaholic. See, you're even thinking about your next takeover right now. The Stanhopes, right? It's in your eyes."

"What?"

"There's a distance about you." She glanced away. "But what do I know?"

She'd seen it. His worst fear, hiding, dodging.

Maybe he was becoming as ruthless as his father.

Deston's hands clenched at the water.

He wouldn't ever be like Edward Rhodes the Third: a hard man mired in family tradition. A man who would stop at nothing to get ahead.

Even his marriage had been nothing more than another merger, and Deston could see how the arrangement ate away at the old guy.

Lila started paddling toward her rock, glancing over her shoulder, pausing before getting out. Modest?

Her shyness prodded him, made him way too damned impetuous—just like he'd been with Juliet Templeton.

"Have dinner with me tonight," he said. A tight laugh followed. "It's one way to get me out of the office."

Lila merely stared at him, brown eyes saucer-like.

"Lila?"

She blinked. After a few seconds, she said, "I've got to go."

"That's right. Your family's leaving. But you could stay behind."

With a flutter of speed, she climbed out of the swimming hole. Then, with her back to him, she grabbed a towel and wrapped it around her body.

Her absence already needled him, twisting in his belly. But why should he care?

"There's a gazebo about a half mile from the big house. I'll have the cooks whip up something for us tonight. At, say, eight?"

She stopped all movement, then retrieved her book and water bottle. "I—"

"—will be there," he finished for her. What the hell? As long as both of them understood that this would be a fling—he couldn't tolerate anything more—no harm would be done.

Lila was fumbling into a pair of threadbare Keds, ignoring him.

"I'm going to wait for you," he said, intrigued by her coyness.

She stepped toward the trees, toward the path back to the main residence area. "Don't wait for me."

"I will."

She shook her head. "Are you really that arrogant?"

"That's how I do business."

"I'm not business." She opened her mouth again, then shut it. With a dismissive gesture, she traipsed into the woods, leaving him alone.

But that was nothing new.

Deston looked in her direction for a few seconds more, then submerged his body underwater again, giving himself to the silence.

Chapter Two

Even now, safely inside her quarters one hour later, Emmy's pulse was still thudding in her ears.

She donned the white baseball cap she usually wore in the kitchen, then blew out an anxious breath. What had she been thinking, leading Deston on like that? There'd been more than one chance to tell him who she was, but she hadn't taken it. She'd been too caught up in all the fantastic possibilities, all the flattery and dreams come true. What girl wouldn't love the opportunity to linger—even briefly—under the attentions of the perfect man?

Not that it mattered anymore. The afternoon had almost burned itself out. She was back to her normal life, and Deston would go back to his after she didn't show up for dinner tonight. After all, how serious could he be about the entire scenario?

Even now she couldn't believe it'd happened.

Emmy found herself smiling like a fool. She'd captured one beautiful moment in time with him, and now she could preserve it, press it between the pages of all her silly romantic wishes.

Really, she hadn't felt so darn giddy since Italy, when she'd first met Paolo while taking a sunset walk along the village streets of Tocchi. But the happiness hadn't lasted. Neither had the illusion of being something more than a menial cook, born to serve.

Par for the course. She didn't wear this "Lila" deception well. It felt like a Halloween costume that was one size too small, cutting off her common sense and dignity.

Dignity? Her giddiness faded. Right. If Emmy had any dignity whatsoever, she'd use the lot of it telling Mama she'd serve in the Rhodes's kitchens only until all their loans were finally paid off. Then she'd move on, away from this life. Away from Deston.

Unfortunately, her own outstanding debts included Mama's life savings, which meant Emmy owed her more than just dollar bills. She hadn't wanted to dig into the "school money" her parents had managed to cultivate, but Mama had insisted, saying that it's what Papa would've expected.

For her to serve the Rhodes household to the best of her ability.

Certainly, there was something to be said about pride in doing your best work, but Emmy wanted to do it in a restaurant of her own. She could just imagine it: Francesca's. Named after Mama. Serving Tuscan-inspired food and spirits.

Another fantasy. Another dream to keep her going.

How could she break Mama's heart by leaving the ranch? By rebelling against a life her family had chosen back in the 1800s when Winston Brown had served Edward Rhodes the First when they'd forged a dynasty here in Texas?

As she left her room and walked the long path to the kitchens, Emmy knew that she'd been born to follow in the footsteps of her legacy. And she'd make the best of it, doing Mama proud, living up to her dad's memory, paying her dues as well as Papa's medical bills and remaining debts.

Bills the Rhodeses had never known about.

The big house—a mansion, to be honest—topped a slight hill overlooking the Medina River in the near distance, the flat grasslands with their scattered oaks and juniper, the steep slopes and canyons. Most of the servants who worked in the house stayed "underground," downstairs, but Emmy was lucky enough to enjoy a cottage located in back of the mansion. It had belonged to her parents, and since Mama was near retirement, she'd allowed Emmy to take it over. A gift to the new cook.

She took a slight detour and wound her way through one of the flower-garden paths. It was something she hadn't done since six years ago, before she'd left for Tocchi, Italy, at age eighteen, where a distant cousin had taken her under her wing to mentor her in cooking. There, she'd worked in their family trattoria for a few years; that is, until she'd met Paolo. After she'd pieced herself back together sufficiently, she'd gone to New York, taken advantage of financial aid and earned a Culinary Arts Diploma at the Institute of Culinary Education.

But now she was home again.

"*Que tal,* baby?" asked a chipper voice.

Emmy smiled at her new visitors. Carlota Verde sashayed into the rose garden, accompanied by her best friend, Felicia Markowski. Both of them worked as maids in the big house. Both of them had grown up with Emmy, too. All of them had nursed crushes on Deston. "The D-Liteful Fan Club" they'd called themselves, scribbling rhyming poetry in their shared diaries, writing letters about ranch life and rumors about the boys once Emmy had left them. They'd also banded together at school to ignore the popular girls with the tight designer jeans and Miss Texas smiles.

Felicia surveyed Emmy, the maid's blond ponytail shimmering in the sun. "Look at her. Em, you got some real sun today."

"I decided to take advantage of the time off before I take over in the kitchens." Emmy's skin doubled in

heat output, and she knew the color of it went way beyond the burn of today's swimming-hole nap.

"Em?" Carlota asked, bending down to catch her
friend's down-turned gaze.

Heck, the stone path had been fascinating. Why did
Carlota have to go and ruin her view?

Big brown sloe eyes narrowed as Carlota led
Emmy's gaze upward once again. "Something's already wrong because you're wearing your oh-oh face."

"Oh-oh as in Italy oh-oh?" Felicia asked.

"Kind of," Emmy said. She frowned, mainly because she knew that if she didn't come out with the
truth now, Carlota was bound to "feel" it anyway. "But
it's nothing I can't nip in the bud. Not like with Paolo."

"Paolo," they both said, shaking their heads. Felicia
slid a compassionate baby-blue gaze over to Emmy.
Carlota, well, she just looked as though she was about
to throttle Emmy for losing her regained strength this
soon.

"I don't need a psychic vision to know where this
is leading," the brunette said.

And she wasn't joking. Carlota was born with the
gift of sight, much to her frequent regret. The girls had
grown up with her eerie portents, her bad nighttime
dreams.

Emmy shifted her stance, tucked her hands into the
pockets of her white cargo pants. "I suppose I've got
another oh-oh situation on the horizon. I ran into Deston today."

"Deston Rhodes," Felicia sighed, ever the romantic optimist.

Carlota shot her an amused look. "So? Tell us everything."

They all drew closer together.

"I was at the old swimming hole, just minding my business, when he rode up on his horse."

"Prince Phillip in *Sleeping Beauty,* finding the princess hidden in the woods. He was lovely," Felicia said.

"He was a cartoon," Carlota said. "Go on, Em."

Emmy didn't take their Deston-drooling very seriously. It'd been more of a bonding exercise for them anyway, until they started getting real boyfriends. She linked arms with Felicia, and the blonde grinned at her.

"He started chatting with me," Emmy said, "as if he was a host at a dinner party making small talk, conducting business."

"Of course," Carlota said. "Even when he's out of the office, he's in it. At least, that's what they say."

"Right. But he sounded as if he knew me already. Called me 'Lemon Face.'"

"So he was obviously romancing you," Carlota said, laughing.

Emmy's cheeks flared with embarrassment, remembrance: The brush of the slight hair on his chest as it whisked against her own skin. His choppy breaths warming her ear. A wish come true, swelled with dangerous hope.

Carlota's mouth gaped. "He *was* romancing you. Is that why you're so glum?"

"It doesn't matter. He thinks I'm Lila. As in Stanhope."

"Wait." Carlota took a step back. "He thought you were one of our ranch guests?"

"Yeah. I guess she was a corporate kid who used to visit."

"Right," Carlota said, voice laced with wariness. "One of *them*."

Her friend still felt the needles of their teasing, too. Could the three of them ever forget? *Your mom scrubs toilets!* they'd yell. *Your dad waits on mine!*

Emmy swallowed. "When Deston sees me around the ranch, he's going to think I'm his childhood 'Lemon Face' and daughter of a bigwig. Just my luck, isn't it?"

"He won't see you around the ranch," Felicia said.

Emmy stared at her friend.

"She's right." Carlota held up a finger. "Number one: He's never here. Well, every once in a while when big Mr. Rhodes requests his presence for a deal, but rarely. Deston lives in San Antonio, in his office. They say that his daddy is sending him to New York soon, too."

Emmy folded her arms over her stomach. "He is?"

"To oversee business there. You have a short window to further this opportunity, Em."

"Not an option." Emmy shook her head. He was

leaving, right when she'd caught his eye? Not that it was relevant, but it was her typical luck with men. And maybe it was for the best, considering her track record.

"And number two…?" Felicia asked.

"When is the last time you saw anyone in the family besides Mrs. Rhodes in the kitchens? Or in the laundry? Or anywhere downstairs? That's why they have Hendrich and Hausfrau Dominatrix," Carlota said, referring to the head butler who'd taken the place of Emmy's father after his death, as well as head of household. For reasons known only to them, the maids called her the Hausfrau Dominatrix rather than her real name, Mrs. Wagner.

"So," Emmy said, somewhat entertained and flattered by their enthusiasm, "if I told you that Deston sort of asked me out, you all would tell me I should go?"

"Emmy? Do you know what this means?" Felicia gave a hop of excitement. "You've done it. You've reached the dream of every girl who grew up staring at Deston with hearts in her eyes, every girl who ever cheered him from the stands. You're a chosen one!"

Emmy narrowed her eyes, though she smiled, as well. "I wouldn't go that far."

"More details," Carlota said, still analyzing the situation. "Fill us in on everything."

It was almost as if someone had taken a little mini Emmy skillet and placed it on a stove, lighting the burner to full flame. The heat came in waves over her body, making her weak, strong, weak.

"He swam in his boxers, and then asked me to dinner. That's all," Emmy said, reluctant to reveal the most intimate details. Something lost and vulnerable told her to keep the skin-on-skin part of it to herself. It was her secret moment, kept in the memory box of her heart, because it'd never happen again.

"Oh," Carlota said, closing her eyes, "I can bet he looked *muy guapo.*" She flapped her hand for emphasis.

They all paused for a moment, allowing Emmy to relive the sight. His cut-muscled torso, tanned and gleaming in the sun. Water darkening his hair, sliding in drops down his full lips, chiseled jaw, neck.

Carlota sighed. "And he thinks you're Lila Stanhope?"

"Yes, he does. I never managed to correct his assumption. I thought it wouldn't go any further than the swimming hole."

And I didn't want to see his disappointment.

"Well," Carlota said, "at least you had a good view of Deston in his boxers. That'll last you for years. And if you go to dinner tonight…"

"You're not serious."

"Em—"

"No," she repeated. "Enough is enough. Dinner's absolutely out of the question."

Felicia held up three fingers, silencing the debate. "There's a number three, you know."

"What?" Carlota said.

"The third reason Emmy doesn't have to worry about Deston discovering who she is." She held up her hands, palms facing the sky. Elementary, my dear girl-friends. "We packed up the Stanhopes this morning. They left about a half hour ago."

Carlota got a scary gleam in her dark eyes. "So with a little adjusting, you can be Lila tonight."

"You all are crazy." Emmy started to walk away. "Mama's expecting me in the kitchen."

"Why *not* do it?" Felicia asked.

"This is ludicrous."

"Hey." Carlota's no-nonsense tone stopped Emmy in her tracks. "Think of how he looked at you."

That did it.

His gaze had meant everything because, in his eyes, she'd felt beautiful. Felt as if she'd walked into a ball wearing a dress that whispered against her skin like stardust. Felt as if she'd been living in a fantasy.

But those never lasted long enough, did they?

Felicia took Emmy by the shoulders. "Did you feel like you were one of them?" Her *them* was more rose-tinged than Carlota's rendition of the word.

Emmy swallowed away the lump in her throat. *One of them.* "I guess I did."

"Then go to dinner," Felicia continued. "You can say that you, Lila, wanted to see him one last time and will join your family tomorrow. Then, in one week, he'll be across the country without ever knowing. No harm done."

"What if he searches her out?"

Carlota waved away the question. "I don't think he will. Remember, he'll be gone in *one week*. Besides, everyone knows that Deston isn't the committing type. He's married to the office. After tonight, you make it clear that it's over. It's just a dinner, after all."

Emmy's heartbeat tripped at the thought of it. This was wrong to even consider.

Yet, what if Felicia and Carlota were right? Emmylou Brown didn't have enough romantic oomph to interest a man long-term anyway, so leaving the romance behind after a limited time wouldn't be a problem. That's how it'd been with Paolo, with every minor boyfriend since.

"He'll never know," Carlota said, wiggling her brows.

"And if you don't do it, you'll be saying, 'I wonder,' for the rest of your life," Felicia added.

They watched her, waiting for an answer, but Emmy had no idea what to say.

Should she go with the flow, treat herself to one night of fun and hope that Deston wouldn't visit the kitchens for the next week?

Or should she play by the rules, stay in her place, live downstairs for the rest of her life?

Confused, she lifted her hand in farewell to her friends. "Mama's waiting. I'll see you all later."

Emmy could feel their eyes on her as she walked to the kitchens.

To where she belonged.

* * *

In the cigar lounge, where Deston had wandered after not eating more than two bites of a tempting dinner, he found himself staring at the wall again.

The Wall of Fame.

Or, as he liked to call it, The Wall of Shame.

The oak paneling featured photographs from days gone by, generations of family accomplishments in black-and-white. Painful color.

Here was a shot of Edward the First posing next to *the* oil well, his mouth in a straight, proud line, his bearded chin lifted, peering down at the camera. Then there were more pictures showing important business acquisitions, significant connections. His granddad posing with Lyndon B. Johnson. His dad playing golf with Papa George Bush. Harry, his brother, stiffly placing his arm around the second President Bush.

And there was Deston. With a football.

The taste of brandied tobacco soured his mouth after he blew out the smoke, turning away from the wall to find his father watching him.

Stark white hair, a full beard, a rounded stomach stuffed full of Texas beef and the best whiskey available. And those penetrating green eyes. How could he forget those eyes? They'd followed him everywhere, from cradle to playing field, from his first acquisition to tonight's silent meal.

They'd even watched him closely after Juliet Templeton had reduced his judgment to ash. After she'd proven to him that he wasn't suited for relationships anyway.

"Your mother's wondering why you didn't eat much," Edward the Third said.

"I'll be going out."

"To a roadhouse?"

Deston puffed on his cigar, took his time blowing out the steam. "Maybe."

That's where he could end up if Lila Stanhope didn't meet him. He'd heard that her family had already left, but that didn't mean she wouldn't come back to the ranch.

Cocky son of a gun. Deston half smiled. Lila hadn't committed to a thing. Still, should he ask Mrs. Wagner to make arrangements with the cook? Something light and quick, since the cuisine wouldn't be the first order of business...?

"I'll see you in hell before you get caught yahooing in a local honky-tonk." Mr. Rhodes settled himself into a leather chair. The room's rustic trappings complemented the man: the tough copper accessories—empty serving trays, tubs filled with herbs, ashtrays; the rough-hewn, hand-carved pine furnishings; the original Remingtons hanging above the fireplace and above a mounted antique saddle.

He seemed so at home.

"Don't worry," Deston said, "I won't tarnish the family name."

That was his brother's area of expertise, Deston realized, hating himself for thinking it—and for admiring Harry because he'd almost gotten away with it.

"Your mother would be devastated." Mr. Rhodes stuck a Cuban cigar into his mouth, flared up a match and lit it. After a few experimental inhalations, he said, "She's over the moon to have you home."

Deston nodded, leaning against the door frame that led out of the room. "It's been a while."

"You should come back here more."

"There's always a lot of work to be done in San Antonio. You know that better than anyone."

Was now the right time to say something about what he'd found yesterday? What he suspected his dad of doing with the Stanhope account?

His father's gaze speared into him, as if he knew. "Out with it, Deston."

He locked gazes with him. A pair of some unfortunate bovine's long horns hovered over Mr. Rhodes, lending him an aggressive air.

"I found records. Numbers. Payments going to people who work for the Stanhopes in different facilities."

His father leaned back in his chair. "That's got your goat?"

"What's the purpose, Dad? I'd like to be in on it, seeing as I'm a CEO."

"It's my area, son. You concern yourself with our New York responsibilities, and I'll take care of this part of the country."

Frustration simmered in Deston's veins, veiling his

sight with a red glow. What was his father doing? Was he sending Deston to New York to hide something?

"It's just odd," Deston said, "that recent mishaps have lowered the value of several Stanhope properties."

"What the hell are you saying?"

Deston stiffened to a defensive stance. "You're going to treat the Stanhopes better than the last ones, right?"

"If you're referring to Endor Incorporated, we both know that was unfortunate."

A competing company had pulled out of the bidding process, leaving Endor in a weakened state of negotiation, vulnerable to the takeover from Rhodes Industries. Deston had his suspicions about the reasons the other corporation had backed off.

But he didn't want to believe any of them.

A muttered curse escaped Deston, causing Mr. Rhodes to laugh.

"Aren't you full of spit and fire?" he asked. "Good. I need you to be my soldier. Harry's got the head for numbers, but no guts. You…"

"Don't depend on it."

"I'd like to." Mr. Rhodes concentrated on snubbing out his cigar in an ashtray. "I sure would've liked you to have met Lila Stanhope."

Deston smothered the spark that jumped to life in his chest. Lila. After she'd gone, he'd spent the next hour swimming off pent-up lust.

Fighting off his longing for more.

Would she be there tonight?

He smashed out his own cigar. "I don't need your matchmaking skills to keep me amused."

"Don't tell me. Work keeps you busy." He stood, patted his ample belly.

Had that been a note of melancholy in his tone? "Someone has to keep Rhodes Industries honest."

His father didn't say a word, just lasered a glare of reproach at his son. Maybe there was even contained respect there, too.

Then he glanced at the Wall of Shame. "No one gets to the top without stepping on a few bodies. That's what it means to be a Rhodes."

Hellfire, if he launched into the "Family and Texas" lecture again, Deston was going to throw rotten tomatoes at him. From day one, the credo had been drilled into him. Family sticks together with an adhesive called pride. And Texas? Hell, every citizen of the greatest state in creation was born with the we're-the-best gene.

That made the Rhodes family doubly arrogant. Juliet had been turned on by the idea of it, but her feelings for him hadn't been strong enough to make her commit to him, to make her be the woman Deston had needed in his life.

And when he'd given her no other choice, he'd lost her. For good.

Deston restlessly moved toward the door. "If you

don't mind, I'll be hitting the roads to search out the sleaziest honky-tonk I can find."

He left the statement hanging, wondering whether his father was in the mood to challenge him or in one of those my-son's-a-star-football-player streaks of indulgence. You never knew with Edward Rhodes.

Not that his blessing mattered.

"Use your head," was all his father said, and as far as Deston was concerned, the statement could be interpreted either way.

But as he left the cigar lounge, he didn't head out of the house. Instead, his steps took him to an almost-hidden door off the foyer which led to elevators that traveled to a place he'd rarely gone before.

The kitchens.

What did Lila like to eat? Would food matter if she showed up tonight?

The service hall got darker as he traveled its length. More foreign. A different world altogether.

He ran into a maid first. When she saw him, she jumped back, dropped the towels she was carrying.

"Mr. Rhodes!" she said, then glanced at the floor.

He hated when they did that. He shifted lower, trying to catch her eye. When that failed, he thought maybe he could say her name to snag her attention. Unfortunately, he was ashamed to admit that he didn't know her name. Didn't know her face.

Truthfully, he didn't know any of them.

Even when he was a kid, the line between the family and the help had been firmly drawn. Once, when he was five, he'd sneaked down to the kitchens, just to grab a snack. The cook—Mrs. Brown?—had given him a biscotti. He still remembered how crunchy and flaky it'd been. But the efficient Mrs. Wagner had caught him down there and had informed his mother.

His brother had told him the cook had been given a "talking to" about spoiling Deston. And Deston himself had been locked in his room for three hours, just to drum the lesson into his skull.

You're a privileged one.

He didn't belong downstairs. Encouraging friendly relations with the help was the sign of a loose household, and the Rhodes clan ran life with an iron fist.

The maid had already scuttled away, so Deston glanced around, finding no one else.

What the hell. Maybe it was time to set things straight around here. Maybe it was time to break the Rhodes mold—both in business and in household.

His parents couldn't lock him in his room now.

Besides, Lila needed something to eat, and he didn't have time to hunt down the proper liaison to get some food around here. It was ridiculous to have to pick up a phone to dial Mrs. Wagner and order the cook to prepare a simple meal.

He'd do it himself.

Deston pressed the button on the wall and waited for the elevator to take him down to the kitchens.

Lila. He hated that he couldn't stop thinking about her.

Hated that he couldn't wait to see her again.

Chapter Three

In the massive, stainless-steel-and-stucco kitchens, Emmy and Francesca Brown were wrapping up their discussion of tomorrow's dinner menu, surrounded by the lingering aroma of the wood-burning oven.

"So there we have it," Francesca said, massaging her hands. Blue veins stood against her browned skin like a string of twilight-smeared hills cresting the land.

Arthritis. It was forcing her out of the job, away from her passion.

Without another thought, Emmy took hold of a hand, rubbed it between her palms. "We start with a Vera Cruz maize tamale for an appetizer, then a salad and shaved fennel/onion bruschetta. Then we've got our moho-bone-in rib-eye steak, which Mr. Rhodes will love because it's beef—"

"He does love his meat." Mama agreed.

"—assorted vegetables—I'll check the garden—and a pumpkin-espresso crème brûlée for dessert." Emmy nursed her mother's other hand without pause. "I can start gathering ingredients, and… What is it, Mama?"

Francesca Brown's eyes were tearing as she watched her daughter minister to her. "Your father would bust his buttons, Emmylou."

Would he? Even after this afternoon? "Well, you-all invested enough money in me, right?"

"*Cara,* it's not merely your job I'm talking about." Mama gave a weak, strained pat to Emmy's arm. "I know being an only child was hard on you, if only because Nigel made no secret about wanting a son to carry on his line of work. Butler to the master of the household."

"Everyone has something that makes them feel special," Emmy said. "Some ride bulls in the rodeo because they're good at it. Some become professional singers because of the applause. Papa had his work to make him feel that way."

"And so do we."

Mama closed her brown eyes, and Emmy knew it was from pain, the frustration of advancing age and a particularly bad arthritis day catching up to her.

Robbing her.

She wished she had desire enough to carry on in her Mama's name. But she'd always wanted more. Had almost gotten it, too, with Paolo. And she wasn't talking about superiority. She longed for respect. Being treasured for what she had to offer the world.

Shaking off the thoughts, Emmy said, "Why don't you go to your room? We've cleaned already. Fritz and I will prep for tomorrow. You rest."

"I'll finish here." Mama's eyes—so much like Emmy's own—opened again. She flicked the backs of her fingers under her chin: Italian for "I'm not interested."

Then, with effort, she tried to tuck a gray lock back into the hairnet holding the chignon she favored. Most of her hair was a rich mahogany hue, but silver had crept in, bit by bit.

Emmy reached out. "Why don't you…"

"No one orders a mama around her kitchen."

It was agonizing to watch her move. She all but creaked as she forced her hands to grab a cloth, to wipe down an expansive counter.

Stubborn woman.

Emmy took the rag from her. "You and Papa. I swear. He wouldn't slow down, either. You know what that got him? Sick. And it got you a bunch of medical bills that insurance didn't cover."

"Ah, the British and their stoic resignation. How I miss it." Mama eyed the rag but didn't try to grab it from her daughter. "Sometimes I wonder if you shouldn't have been raised with more of your papa's English calm and less of my village's fire. You All-American melting pots don't respect your elders like we did."

Emmy patted Mama's cheek. "I missed you, even if you're still too hard-headed to let the Rhodes know about all of Papa's debts."

"Not a word, Emmylou—"

A dish broke in the hallway, near the elevator.

Mama mock-growled then aimed her voice in that direction. "Fritz, if that's the Delft china, I'll sauté you in olive oil."

The assistant's flustered words stumbled over apologies until a more masculine voice overrode him.

"My fault," said a deep, unFritz-like drawl. "Is there a broom around here?"

Emmy's joints froze. She'd heard that voice before. This afternoon.

At the swimming hole.

"I'm…going to the gardens," Emmy said, surprised she had enough breath to form a sentence. Her heartbeat nickered and stomped through her limbs, stalling movement until she finally darted away.

"Emmy!" she heard her mama say. "Go in the morning. Emmy?"

Deston. What was he doing down here? Rhodes boys weren't allowed in the kitchens. Everyone knew that.

Except him, obviously.

And wouldn't you know it? He was by the elevators. But she could take the stairs and escape, couldn't she?

She heard Fritz scuttling through the kitchens, probably in search of that broom, then the clinking sound of broken china being swept across the floor.

Deston's voice again. Nearer.

Emmy crouched into the pantry, close enough to catch his words, far enough so that she wouldn't have to face him.

"Mrs. Brown," he said. She could imagine him dressed for dinner, maybe in a business suit with his jacket draped over those expansive shoulders. The Rhodes clan had a dress code, and everyone obeyed it.

"Mr. Rhodes." Mama laughed. Her smile was most likely shining throughout the room. "I haven't seen you since you were, oh, so high."

"Can't say I've been around much." Was his hair tussled from this afternoon's swim? Or had he combed it back into that spiky excuse for a hairdo? "How's the family?"

"Fine, thank you, sir. My Emmylou's back from her studies. She'll be taking over as soon as I can bring myself to let her."

"Emmylou." From the way he said it, she knew he had no idea who she was.

Good.

And bad.

Her mama obviously caught the hint, too. "What brings you to the kitchens? Was dinner satisfactory?"

"It was exceptional. I don't mean to upset the norm," he said, no doubt flashing that charming grin, "but I couldn't find Mrs. Wagner, and I'm short on time for the request I'm about to make."

"Yes, sir?"

Emmy's pulse thudded, consuming her, making it hard to hear. She clutched the edge of a shelf to keep her balance.

"Would it be possible to round up a meal for two? Nothing fancy, because I know whatever you have will be more than adequate."

She held her breath, but the pressure was likely to make her head explode. Was this Lila's meal? *Her* meal?

"Consider it done," Mama said.

"If you have anything left from tonight's dinner, that would do nicely."

Leftovers? She was a leftover kind of girl? Well.

Or maybe he was staring at her mother's hands, knowing the care and pain that went into every meal, wanting to save her the extra work.

Yeah. That was more like Deston. The one she'd worshipped from afar all those years ago.

Er, hours ago.

"Your girlfriend," Mama said, "does she like crab cakes and beef in the potato jackets? The peas à la *française* and gratin of pasta…?"

Enough, Mama.

"She just might, Mrs. Brown." He sounded as though he was enjoying himself.

"She's *bella,* I'll bet. Beautiful."

Oh, boy.

There was a pause, and Emmy wondered if he was finding a way to describe what he'd seen in her. A girl with a tight, timeworn top and cut-off jeans. The girl Paolo had brought to a family dinner only to have his mother take her aside during cocktails on their crumbling balcony to say that her "type" wasn't welcome in the Amati household.

Her type.

Emmy knew she wasn't anything to shout about, but it would still hurt to hear it from Deston's mouth.

Finally, he spoke, his voice lowered, almost strangled. "There's not a word strong enough to describe her. Words don't do her justice. Her smile…" He trailed off.

Emmy sank all the way to the floor, flattened, mind a whir of disbelief. They'd been at the same swimming hole today, right? This *was* the Deston she'd met? And he'd been looking at her smile? Her slightly crooked teeth?

"Good," her mama said, clearly pleased that her employer was happy. "I'll have it prepared in no time for you."

"Much obliged."

"Fritz will run it upstairs, sir."

"I'd appreciate it if he could bring the food to the old gazebo. Would that be too much to ask?"

"Not at all."

"Thank you, Mrs. Brown." Booted footsteps retreated on the linoleum, but Emmy waited until she had herself under control. Relatively.

He was going out to that gazebo to wait for her, as promised. It'd be eight o'clock, and Deston Rhodes would be sitting by himself, a fine meal in front of him, waiting for a date who wouldn't materialize.

He *had* been serious about being there.

Oh, this was worse than allowing him to think she was Lila. Wasn't it?

Maybe she should at least go out there to tell him the truth, no matter how disgusted he'd be. She could tolerate feeling like a servant more than knowing he was going to be stood up by a woman who didn't seem to care.

Because she did care.

She stood, holding on to the wall until her knees stopped shaking. It'd only be one night.

One harmless night of making him laugh as he had at the swimming hole. She craved the feel of that laugh. But then it would be over, and maybe she wouldn't even have to reveal herself. Both of them could avoid embarrassment if she played her cards right.

Yet that's what she'd said about Paolo, too, and look how *that* had ended up.

But Deston… Out there all alone… The food cooling, neglected… She could almost imagine him snuffing out the tabletop candle, lonely, ignored.

Maybe hiding in the kitchens for one week—if Deston could manage to stay out of them—would be a small price to pay for keeping him happy.

Because, after all, that's why she was here. To make the Rhodes family happy.

It was as if Deston had hung the full moon in the blackened sky, along with the lit rusted lanterns that lined the pine gazebo.

Crickets and night creatures provided the music, and Mrs. Brown had supplied the food that he'd spread over the knobby oak table in the center of the structure. A bench encircled the perimeter, but Deston had liberated a couple of upholstered chairs from the storage room and into his truck, hauling them out here.

Now all he needed was Lila.

He checked his watch. Eight-fifteen. She was standing him up, wasn't she?

Pacing, his boots marking each passing second, Deston punched a pole with the heel of his hand as he walked by. Dammit. It wasn't supposed to go like this.

Juliet had been a free spirit, frequently scattering all his best-laid plans. She'd been *too* free; she'd drink an excess of champagne at family functions or forgo the designer dresses he bought for her in favor of what she called "hoochie rags." After her accident, Deston had vowed never to be serious about a woman again. He couldn't live through another tragedy like Juliet.

Love had torn him apart once, and all he wanted now was something simple. Easy.

But had he misread Lila's signals, thinking she might want the same? Hadn't she fitted herself against him, her brown eyes glazed with a yearning that echoed his own?

He leaned against the pole he'd punched, wondering how long he'd stay out here and court his cautious hope.

For a moment, the crickets stopped their singing. The grass rustled with a heavier cadence, and waning heat hung in the stillness of the dark.

"Don't be mad," said her voice.

Deston's veins tangled with the jump of his blood as he whipped around.

She wore a pink sundress, the skirt flowing around her ankles in the slight wind, the color bringing a glow to her sun-flushed olive skin. She'd tucked the front strands of her hair, the blond ones, behind her ears, emphasizing her heart-shaped face. A golden locket hung around her neck, catching the subdued light.

For a second, a greeting, a whiplash remark, caught in his throat and ached there. The tight heat slid down to his chest.

To his belly. Clutching. Conquering.

She moved closer, each step offering more details in the lantern light, revealing nuances like the subtle almond slant of her eyes.

"Deston?"

The fist of longing in his belly tore at him.

Another foot forward. "I didn't know if I'd come tonight."

"Well, you made me wonder for fifteen minutes." There. Back in control, where he belonged.

"Right." She smiled. It wasn't the glimmering flash of high noon he'd seen at the pond, but a sad smile. "Quite a stickler for punctuality, aren't you?"

"Yeah. I'm a real taskmaster." He extended a hand, palm up. "Why don't you come up here?"

She hesitated. "I want you to understand something first. I'm here for one night, a dinner, and then no more. I go back to work after that."

Mr. Stanhope was known for his demands on his children, so her statement didn't surprise him. In fact, it bonded him to her in a small way. "Your dad sounds like a tough boss."

"Yes," she said, glancing away. "He is. But I love him more than anything."

Usually Deston could have a woman in his arms within the first five minutes. Her reluctance frustrated him, intrigued him.

He beckoned with a finger, a tacit command. "You coming or not?"

From beneath her long lashes, she glanced up at him, then accepted his grip. At first touch, awareness exploded through him, rocking the foundations of his strength, its fire licking below his skin, threatening to burn out of reach. Her hand was so tiny in his, so slender. As he lifted her fingers, cupping them over the ridge of his index finger, he noticed that her nails were short, practical.

She must've seen the realization on his face, because she tugged her hand away. But he was too quick, clasping her fingers in his, using his thumb to rub her knuckles.

"Why are you afraid of me?" he asked.

"Afraid?" She laughed, but it was shaky, unsure. "I'm not afraid."

He drew her hand closer to his mouth, rested his lips against her skin. Beneath a cover of sweet-scented lotion—apricots?—he caught the earthy aroma of chives, garlic, pepper. The mixture confused his senses, consuming him.

"You cook."

She laughed again, tightening her hold on him. "I'm staying with a nearby friend, and we whipped something up for a midday snack."

Suddenly, she pulled her grip out of his and sat in one of the chairs. Was she frowning?

"So," she continued, stiffening in her seat, a smile wobbling on her face. "What's for dinner?"

The gesture still wasn't as bright as this afternoon. Not by a long shot.

"You planning to eat and run?" he asked, sitting opposite her.

"It depends on the company, I suppose." With

cheeky grace, she took her napkin, fanned it out, settled it over her lap.

He couldn't help chuckling. "I'll try to keep you entertained. Wouldn't want you making that lemon face, now, would we?"

"Could you please not call me that?"

"Lemon Face? It's got an endearing ring to it."

"It's..." She fidgeted with the stem of her wineglass. Was she nervous? "I've gone beyond such nicknames."

"What should I call you then?"

You could have filled the resulting pause with a truckload of gravel.

She exhaled, shoulders sinking. Deston couldn't identify her expression. Disappointment? Her own brand of frustration? Why?

"Hey, now," he said. "I promise. No more Lemon Face."

A smile fought its way onto her lips, suffusing the night with her glow. *The* smile.

Her teeth were slightly off-kilter, and a gentleness wrapped around his heart, squeezing it. He wondered why she'd never gotten braces, but didn't want to chase away her happiness by asking. Instead, he said, "Sunny."

She cocked an eyebrow. "What?"

"That's what I'll call you from now on. Sunny."

As she stared at him, Deston wanted to roll his eyes at his inner cornball. Could that have been dopier?

To erase the tension, he reached for the uncorked cabernet sauvignon, poured some into her glass, then his.

They both sipped for a moment. You know, maybe the nickname thing was a blessing in disguise. If he didn't think of her as Lila, then maybe he could convince himself that he hadn't fallen right into his father's trap of courting the business associate's daughter.

Maybe he could fool himself just for tonight, guard himself with delusion.

He served all the food courses at once, not sure which came first. But Sunny—it was a good nickname, Sunny—didn't seem to mind. She ate her food, clearly enjoying it, then lifting her face to an unexpected gust of wind as it whistled between them. One lantern guttered out, but she still shimmered.

"We've got some champion cooks here at Oakvale," he said, gesturing toward the meal.

It took her a long time to swallow, so she nodded in answer, gaze on her plate.

Then she cleared her throat, glancing at him again. "So you don't come to the ranch much?"

"No. I'd like to but…"

"Business," she finished for him, then shrugged. "It's a shame. This is what heaven must look like."

From that point on, they polished off Mrs. Brown's cooking in companionable silence, then they small-talked. But all he wanted to do was touch her again, to make use of this one night.

He pushed away his empty plate, his appetite satisfied in one sense.

But not the other.

His gaze roamed over her as she dabbed her mouth with the napkin.

"I should enjoy the ranch while I can," he said, trying to ignore the fullness of her lips and what they'd taste like. "Harry's going to inherit it. I get some corporate holdings."

"You sound a little angry about that."

"Angry?" Him?

Maybe he was.

He continued after a moment. "Harry isn't into the whole 'cowboy crapola,' as he calls it. He's more of a tie-and-jacket kind of guy."

"You can't buy the ranch from him?"

"And break the chain of inheritance?" His laugh was sawgrass-mean. "We've got a little something around here called tradition. You don't mess with it."

Sunny's eyes dimmed with a faraway glaze. "I understand."

How could anyone? "Sometimes I think my family's archaic in so many ways. But patterns are what keep my father sane."

She nodded, leaning on her elbows, propping the side of her head on one hand until she was watching him with the innocence of a little girl falling asleep in front of the fire on Christmas Eve.

"Where are you going to live?" she asked. "After you get kicked out of here, I mean."

"New York. I'm relocating soon."

The statement poised over them, sharp and knife-like. She blinked, and the threat vanished. "So you'll be saying goodbye to the ranch that soon, huh?"

"I don't see anyone around here much anyway."

The flame from a stalwart lantern that had braved the wind flickered in her dark eyes. He moved the wine bottle, leaned closer to her over the intimate table.

"Sunny?" he said.

At first she didn't answer him, just smiled dreamily as he drew nearer. Then she sighed, closed her eyes. Opened them.

"Deston, I—"

"You're beautiful."

She froze, bit her lip.

Damn. Where had that come from? He hadn't meant to bust right out with such naked words. It was fine for a man to think them, but never to admit it.

He cleared his throat. "What I meant to say is that you look a whole lot younger than your age. Our age. You keep well."

Good save.

"No one's ever said that to me before." Her gaze had gone misty. "The beautiful part."

Her voice was as wobbly as that verbal worm he'd just choked up.

"Well," he said, "maybe they should have."

"Boy." She sighed again, more heavily this time, and placed her hands on the edge of the table, shaking her head. "I wish you hadn't said that."

He could only stare. Women were a complete mystery.

Then she aimed her gaze skyward, lifting up her hands in a helpless gesture. "You make this so hard."

He couldn't agree more. Would one night be enough to get his fill of this woman?

Sure, it would. He'd move on, as always, even if there was something about her that made a spark of tenderness flash over his conscience.

Standing, he pointed toward the deserted dude cabins in the near distance. "Maybe we could take a walk."

At first, Sunny seemed confused, then comprehension dawned as she took in the structures, the heat of his gaze.

"Deston, I... Not tonight."

"Then come back tomorrow. Meet me over there, in cabin number five. Same time."

She started to shake her head more emphatically. "You don't understand."

So sweet, so gentle. He wanted to capture the emotions, to hold on to them.

In three strides he was at her side, lifting her out of her chair until he'd crushed her against his chest, one hand planted in her hair, one hand pressing the small of her back until she was melded against him. Her eyes were wide, doe-like.

As wary and willing as he was.

"You're right," he said, his lips whispering against hers. "I don't understand any of this. But you're going to be there. Just like you came to me tonight."

Her heartbeat punched against his chest, echoing the rhythm of his own desires.

"But…"

He didn't let her finish, because he was already kissing her, melting against her with the liquid hunger of something stronger than lust.

Chapter Four

Even while it was happening, Emmy couldn't bring herself to believe it.

Deston Rhodes was kissing her.

Her pulse fluttered madly, robbing her of oxygen, making her head swim with the whirlpool-dizziness of every daydream she'd treasured.

How many times had she imagined this?

There had been hazy goodnight kisses on porches. Kisses where he'd caressed the back of her hand with his lips. Kisses where he'd dipped her over the crook of his strong arm on an elegant dance floor somewhere in Europe, softly fitting his mouth over hers.

But this kiss exceeded all the dreams.

One of his hands was caught in her hair, his palm open to cup her head, cradling it as her neck lost strength and arched back so she could meet his mouth. His other hand nestled in the small of her back, fingers pressing upward, urging her against his long, hard body.

With a lazy, yearning rhythm, he sipped at her. She responded in kind, moaning a little, skimming both her hands under his dinner jacket, up the muscles of his back, clutching him to make up for the strength he was stealing.

Her legs could barely hold her up; they were liquefied like dripping wax. Flame burned her from the inside out, and she felt consumed, reduced to a pliant puddle.

One night of his kisses.

Blazing heat scorched through her, and she parted her lips, welcoming him. He swept his tongue inside her mouth, and she echoed each sultry stroke, tasting traces of wine and spices from their meal.

He came up for air, resting his lips near her ear. "Sunny," he said, the name skimming her skin.

Who? she wanted to ask.

In her dreams, she was still Emmylou Brown, the woman Deston loved no matter what she did for a living.

"Don't say anything," she said, needing to preserve the silence, the innocent lies.

Emmy rubbed her cheek against his, feeling the

slight, harsh rasp of emerging whiskers. In response, he tightened his grip and pulled her closer, bringing her flush against the length of his body.

A ridge of arousal brushed against her belly, and Emmy's blood pounded downward to beat between her legs.

"Does that say enough?" he whispered.

Emmy's brain wasn't working. Her common sense had already been doused by Deston's persuasive touch.

"You told me…" She paused, catching her breath. Her pulse was driving adrenaline through her veins, making her weak. "You're going to New York."

"Exactly."

He skimmed his fingertips up her spine, traveling the zipper of her sundress. Then he paused at the top, toying with the tab.

A wham-bam night of fun? That's what he was proposing.

While his fingers busied themselves at her nape, he formed kisses with each word, branding her neck with suggestions.

"What's…the…harm?" he asked.

She sighed and lifted up her chin, allowing him access to the sensitive dip that separated her collarbones. He swirled his tongue into it, then upward, coasting his lower lips to her jaw.

Not that she was thinking clearly right now, but what *was* the harm? She'd live a dream come true, and he'd go away happy, never the wiser.

It wasn't as if she was putting her heart on the line, as she'd done with Paolo. This was a simple deal.

A one-night stand.

But the phrase didn't sit right with her.

Air tickled her nape as he deliberately undid her zipper an inch.

"Deston…"

"I want to see you. All of you."

"I…"

"At the swimming hole today, I imagined what you'd look like without those clothes."

Emmy flushed as she remembered how her thin top had clung to her breasts, no doubt making his fantasy session pretty easy.

During her pause, he nudged the zipper down an inch lower. Her sundress peeled open a little, leaving the center of her back exposed.

She shivered. "Are you this successful with all the girls?"

She felt the shape of his mouth turn into a smile against her skin, just below her jaw.

"I wouldn't say I've reached my goal with you just yet."

Deston Rhodes really did want her. Or who he thought was her, at least.

Did that make her crave more? Or were kisses enough?

He sucked her earlobe into his mouth, and Emmy

just about collapsed, grabbing onto him for more support. In answer, he shifted against her, still aroused.

Maybe this was too real. Maybe she just wanted Deston to stay the way she'd always imagined him: slightly out of reach, inaccessible, a golden boy touched by the sun.

Instinctively, she braced her hands against his chest and gently pushed away. She could feel his surprise, disappointment—whatever it was that straightened his spine.

With a gruff sigh, he leaned his forehead against hers, zipping her back up.

"Too fast," she said, adding a laugh to ease the tension.

"The pace was fine by me."

He hadn't let go of her. Instead, he was rubbing his palms up and down her arms.

"Goosebumps," she said. "Right in the middle of summer, too."

"Are you cold?" He slipped out of his dinner jacket and spread it over her shoulders, giving the lapels one final tug before he moved back.

"Thank you." Emmy couldn't look in his eyes, just as Paolo hadn't been able to look into hers after his mom had kicked Emmy out of their villa.

Not that she'd done anything as remotely vile as Paolo had. She wouldn't ever take advantage of a man she professed to love, then turn him away.

No, this wasn't the same situation at all. Where

Paolo had carelessly used her body, Emmy had actual feelings for Deston. As much as she could have after knowing him for an afternoon, and after leading him to think she was someone else and then gleaning information about the real Lila from her best friends.

Emmy gulped. That's right. She'd prepared herself with a smattering of Lila's personal information, just in case. But she didn't intend to use any of it.

Did that make her any different from the man who'd broken her own heart a few years ago? Was she also a lying jerk?

Deston reached out to crook a finger under her chin, guiding her face up to meet his gaze. "You're sad."

She thought about the days after Paolo had left her. The days when her elder Italian cousin had lectured about earning a spot as the local tramp. The days when she couldn't even walk down the hill to the market without hearing the nasty comments from boys who loitered on stairways, the judgmental glares from women taking cappuccino on the *terrazzas*.

"I'm only confused," Emmy said, trying to smile, hoping he wasn't angry because she'd ended their embrace.

"Confused about being with me? Why?"

She paused. Sunny. Lila. Emmy the cook.

With infinite gentleness, he cupped her face in his hands. "I can't apologize for wanting you so badly."

Why did he have to go and be so sweet? She didn't *want* to tell him the truth.

"Besides," he said, sliding his hands down her neck, her collarbone, over the necklace decorating her upper chest. His fingers lingered just above the plunge of her dress. "It's not like I'm asking for your hand in marriage."

Emmy's romantic bubble wobbled.

His green eyes gleamed wickedly as he skimmed his knuckles over her breasts, causing them to strain against the cotton, peaking.

"I only want the here and now," he finished, smoothing his hands over her waist to draw her closer again.

Paolo had desired her, too. He'd come from a wealthy family who'd seen better times, had believed he was entitled to everything in the village because they were determined to be rich again. If she'd known he was such a creep, she wouldn't have given him the time of day. But Paolo had been blessed with a silver tongue, had whispered such words of encouragement that Emmy had conjured thoughts of marriage and forever when all he'd really wanted was a mistress.

Upstairs people. Maybe they were all the same deep down.

Arrogant. Greedy.

Maybe, with folks like Paolo and Deston, there could never be anything more than short-term.

I'm not an invisible servant, she thought, driven by memory. I've got needs, too.

"So I should live for the moment with you?" she

asked, voice tight with something close to resentment. "That's all?"

"That's all I can handle, darlin'."

Emmy stared at him a moment longer. Then, driven by desire and hurt, she grabbed the back of his head, guiding him to her, claiming his lips with her own, letting him know that *she* could take what she wanted, too.

Deston's gut gave a heated lurch as she plunged her tongue into his mouth, rampaging, flirting with every ounce of his control. He fought to keep from sliding her to the gazebo floor, cushioning her with his arms, filling her with an erection that was even now throbbing for release.

Instead, he slowed the pace of the kiss while she fought to keep it wild.

A flash of memory exploded in his mind. Juliet. Party-girl Juliet Templeton. She'd kissed him with such fire, too.

The reminder singed him.

"Sunny…" he managed to say.

She took his lower lip between both of hers, sucked on it, slowly let it slide out of her mouth with a final, saucy caress. Her brown eyes were shaded, hiding something from him.

Had he offended her with his honesty?

Maybe so. But what else could he do? Deston was never going to fall in love again. Why pretend otherwise?

She shrugged out of his coat and presented it to him. "I've got to go."

"It's early." Was she really leaving?

"Better than too late." She stepped toward the stairs. "I appreciate the dinner. Do you need—"

She stopped herself, shaking her head. "I suppose you've got servants to clean up our mess."

"I'm sorry if I insulted you, Sunny, but I'm not one to deceive a woman about my lifestyle. I thought from the way you acted at the swimming hole today that you'd be open to…well, whatever might've happened tonight."

Silence.

As she placed a hand against a gazebo pole, Deston wanted to pull her back into his arms.

How had such a good night gone bad?

The wind picked up. Sunny lifted her head to the gust, then smiled. "Have a safe trip to New York, okay? And do me a favor. Don't mention this to anyone."

"If that's what you want." He moved toward her.

She didn't flinch. "I appreciate your discretion."

"Too bad it's wasted."

Hesitating, she parted her lips as if to answer, then fled the gazebo, her pink skirt flaring around her knees, making him think of a whirlwind spinning away from him.

"Sunny."

She stopped, her skirt blowing against those slim legs as she peeked back over her moon-bathed shoulder.

Deston's palm ached from wanting to feel her smooth skin again. "I meant what I said about tomorrow night. Cabin number five. I'm going to be there."

"I won't."

"That's what you said today."

She shook her head. "No good will come of us meeting up again."

"It's a chance worth taking."

Sunny plucked at her dress, then turned her back on him, walking away, speeding her pace until she was holding her skirt, running.

Deston watched her until she disappeared into the night.

He'd see if she came tomorrow. If not, he'd move on. It was that simple.

Wasn't it?

The next morning, Emmy stabbed at the vegetable garden dirt with a spade, transplanting leeks.

Felicia was right next to her, struggling to wrap Emmy in some exotic swath that covered most of her wide-brimmed hat and face. According to Felicia's new plan, sunglasses, gardening gloves and baggy clothing should swallow the rest of Emmy, hiding her just in case Deston was roaming the grounds.

Rumor had it that the young Mr. Rhodes was making an odd effort to put names to the servants' faces this morning, so Felicia thought it prudent to take action, just in case he came upon them. Generally though, the help couldn't wait until big Mr. Rhodes and Mrs. Rhodes found out about Deston's downstairs wanderings. Really, drama was at a premium in the house right now, ever since Harry Rhodes had married and moved out.

Even more interesting, rumor also had it that Deston had slyly hired a cleaning crew from San Antonio to come in and polish some of the dude cabins from top to bottom.

Emmy worked at another leek, releasing her anxiety. She'd refused his invitation last night, if she wasn't mistaken. Hadn't she been clear about her intentions to stay away from him?

After she'd lost her temper, rocking his world with that last you-can't-have-everything-rich-boy kiss and leaving him puzzled, she hadn't expected him to carry on with plans for cabin number five tonight.

Stubborn mule.

"Stay still," Felicia said. She was also dressed in what Emmy called "beekeeper garb."

Felicia accidentally stuffed the material in Emmy's mouth while trying to wrap it around her head. Finally, she secured it.

"Just wait," she said, chipper as ever. "You'll thank me for taking no chances. Besides, you don't need more sun. I didn't think someone with your skin could burn so easily."

"I didn't burn," Emmy said, holding out a completely covered arm. "I tanned. Yesterday's overindulgence has already turned into a nice, even bake."

"You're trying to make me jealous. So, I'm pale and burn easily. It can't be helped. I've got my dad's Polish blood and my mom's German skin."

Like Felicia, Emmy was also an ethnic "melting pot." Mama had met Emmy's British-American father at a Wycliffe wedding for mutual friends during the early eighties. At that point, Francesca had been an exchange student from Italy. Not long afterward, she and Nigel had tied the knot and later she'd given birth to their all-American girl.

A well-wrapped Felicia took a seat on a nearby bench and cracked open her journal, tolerating the outdoors just to be with her newly returned friend during her own day off.

"Dear Diary," Emmy said, laughing. "What's the big news today, Felicia?"

"I'm writing about Toby, of course."

"Oh, yes, the rodeo cowboy. Can't wait to meet him."

"He's a good guy. I think, this time, we're going somewhere. No more dead-end relationships for me."

Emmy transplanted the last leek and put her spade in her equipment basket. "Does he know?"

Felicia shook her head. "Might as well leave the bombshell for when things progress. I don't want to scare him away yet."

"If he's frightened, then he doesn't deserve you. Forget any man who can't love you the way you are."

The forced smile on her friend's face didn't fool Emmy. Felicia couldn't have children, and the fact had put a strain on all of her budding relationships.

"Wouldn't it be nice," Emmy continued, "if the real you didn't matter to this guy?"

"Sounds like you've been thinking about the subject."

"Especially after last night. Deep in my heart, I wanted to drive Deston crazy with passion, and that's what happened. He just isn't crazy about *me*."

"Yes, he is." Felicia snapped her journal shut. "He wants *you*, Em. He doesn't even know this Lila."

"Still, he calls me by a different name. But that's my fault." Emmy crushed a clod of dirt between her gloved fingers. "Funny, how I like him and don't like him at the same time. When I heard him saying, 'I want this,' 'I want that,' 'I want you just for one night,' Paolo came back to haunt me. So did the voices of all the house guests, demanding things."

"You sound a little angry."

"I'm not."

Emmy tossed the dirt away.

"Em, Paolo was a first-class cretin. We both know that. He made you think there was a chance with him, then let his mommy do the dirty work and make the break with you. He always knew you'd be turned away from his family." Felicia hmphed. "Gold-digger. I'll bet he's married to a bored rich woman who could refill his family's coffers. Someone with the pedigree of Mrs. Rhodes."

"Do you think it's that bad between them? The Mr. and Mrs.?"

"Oh, yeah. You know how you notice subtle things as you get older? Things like how small your old school room really is, how your parents don't know everything? The Mr. and Mrs. haven't really talked for the past few years. They sleep in separate bedrooms now."

Once again, Deston's one-night-only request hit Emmy in the heart. Did his parents' relationship affect the way he saw love?

"Be that as it may, I'm in too deep already," Emmy said. "I may have had a magic night, but I'm not seeing Deston again."

Felicia didn't say a word, knowing better than to talk Emmy into anything.

In silence, the friends went about their tasks. Felicia no doubt scribbled optimistic notations about Toby while Emmy shifted over to a staked tomato plant to select the juiciest vegetables from the vine. She wanted to experiment with a marinara sauce this afternoon, one she'd been working on for months now, but she couldn't get the spices right.

Well, she'd try anyway. Never give up, she always said. Never turn away from what you really want.

"Oh, oh," Felicia said, catching Emmy's attention.

"What's wrong?"

"Don't act flustered, okay, Em?"

Her stomach did a cartwheel. "He's coming, isn't he?"

"He's walking toward us. Just... I don't know. Keep your head down." Felicia stood, smoothed the nonexistent wrinkles from her sun-sheltered ensemble. "I knew it. Didn't I tell you these clothes would come in handy? And think about the benefits to your skin."

From beneath her sunglasses, Emmy peered toward the big house, where Deston was indeed headed toward them. Garbed in faded jeans, boots and that Stetson, he made her sigh in wistful appreciation.

She adjusted her glasses. Did she have time to run again?

Something inside her got all riled up, refusing to flee. She'd done it too many times. Once with Paolo, and last night with Deston.

She hated to be that kind of person.

Felicia fidgeted as he approached. "I don't know why Deston's making nice with the help, especially since Harry will be the one living here some day."

"How gracious of him." And all the kind, big-hearted rich people.

Yet in spite of her judgment, she couldn't help admiring the gesture. Why had he decided to care?

She heard the brusque cadence of his boots on the flagstone before he actually arrived. Felicia smiled at him.

"Emmy?" he asked, extending his hand toward the blonde.

"No, sir." She glanced at his outstretched palm as

if it were a stick of dynamite, then cautiously shook it. "I'm Felicia Markowski. Housekeeping."

"Well, no wonder the place looks so tidy. You don't have a wrinkle on you."

Even under all the material, Emmy could see that Felicia was glowing. "Thank you, Mr. Rhodes."

"Mrs. Brown told me her daughter's in the gardens somewhere. I'd like to meet her, too."

Her guts seized up. This wasn't good.

"Er… You know, I think Em's…"

One, two, three… Emmy poked her head out from behind the tomato plant. With a stiff wave—she made sure it was very unSunny-like—Emmy ducked behind her mouth-wrapping and pointed to her throat. Then she shrugged.

"Em…lost her voice," Felicia said, catching on quickly. "She screamed so loudly at her going-away party in New York that she can't talk. And she's got this skin condition, too. When she's in the sun, it's bad news."

Deston took a step toward Emmy, craning his neck to get a better look at her. She retreated behind the plant, busying herself with more plucking.

"I'm no stranger to the city," he said. "Ms. Brown, maybe we can talk about your adventures there one day?"

Oh, brother.

Felicia interrupted. "She'd rather forget she ever saw the place, if you don't mind, Mr. Rhodes. Em's really sensitive about what happened there."

Great, Felicia, thought Emmy. Go ahead and be melodramatic.

"In that case," he said, "I'll cut to the chase."

He approached the row where Emmy was working, and she turned her back to him, assuming a slouched posture a woman like Sunny wouldn't be caught dead in. She could hear Felicia tracking him.

"Ms. Brown, I've come to ask you a favor."

Felicia came to stand over her. "I can translate."

Emmy's heart warmed at her friend's protective efforts, just as her body temperature was rising—burning, actually—at Deston's proximity.

Last night's honeyed whispers.

Demanding kisses.

Emmy's hands quaked as she tried to contain herself.

"Translation? Fair enough," Deston said, his voice sounding distant, a bit preoccupied. "Ms. Brown, I was wondering if you could help me with…well, a sort of special event tonight."

Cabin five. He was still planning to meet his Sunny.

Deston continued. "Your mother suggested your favorites—scalloped tomatoes with pearl onions, saffron risotto and chicken Marsala—nothing too complicated. But she said your Italian meal would impress the person I'm entertaining."

He wanted to impress *her*. Emmy's heart gave a happy leap.

Unbelievable. She was special enough to merit her own delicious meal.

With a brusque, impulsive nod, Emmy signaled Felicia that she'd do it. It was her job, after all. She was surprised he was even out here *asking* for her to do it.

Wait. Was she going to cook the meal then not show up? Abort mission. Abort mission!

"This must be some truly wonderful company," Felicia said, "if you don't mind me saying so, Mr. Rhodes. But you didn't have to hire a crew from outside Oakvale to clean those cabins when you have staff here."

Emmy wanted to tug on Felicia's long skirt to remind her that they wanted him to leave as soon as possible.

"I guess I can't hide it from anyone. This is an important night." She could hear the smile in Deston's voice. But then he cleared his throat. "It's all about business though. And the housekeeping crew has enough to do without traipsing out to those cabins."

So she was business? Did he schedule his lovemaking like his board meetings?

Maybe…just maybe…he didn't want anyone to know about Sunny. Maybe he was discreet, too.

Still, his tone had changed when he'd said he couldn't hide "it" from anyone. What was "it" exactly?

Emmy chanced a glance up at him. His tall form was half-shadowed in the lenses of her sunglasses, but she could see the hope in the grin he fought, in the way he sheepishly hooked his fingers in the pockets of his jeans.

Awww. What was he doing to her?

Shoot. She shouldn't go. She'd had her fantasy Deston kiss, a beautiful lantern-lit dinner.

An excited little voice inside her head asked, *But why should you stop there?*

Yeah. Why?

If Emmy didn't meet him tonight—just one more night, and that was definitely it—she'd be calling herself a fool for the rest of her life.

Deston caught her gaze, and she gulped, hoping her shapeless garb was enough to keep her identity hidden.

"Would a seven o'clock dinner be enough notice for you, Ms. Brown?"

Emmy gave a creaky nod, again taking care to avoid any Sunny-isms.

"Great."

"Believe me, Mr. Rhodes," Felicia said, "Em will be more than happy to have her stuff there by seven."

Her "stuff." Emmy was going to get Felicia back for her playfulness. Right after she pulled her heart from her throat and put it back into her chest.

"Much obliged." Deston started to leave. "Nice to meet you all."

And, with a lingering glance at Emmy, then a nod, he left them. This time, she couldn't help leaning around the plant to catch sight of him.

Boy, those jeans were made to cling to his long legs, his perfect—

"'But I'm not seeing Deston again,'" Felicia teased, imitating Emmy.

"What am I doing, Felicia?"

"Chasing a dream. And unlike most people on earth, you're going to catch it."

"I'm going on the down escalator to hell for this."

"Don't say that. You'll be with him tonight and then, bam! He's gone." Felicia bent down, clasped Emmy's hands in hers. "Take it from me. We always hear the rumors about Deston and how he can't settle down. As long as you're okay with the situation, you've got nothing to lose."

Except her self-respect.

Even so, Emmy wanted to go to cabin five tonight, just to see what would happen. To hear him whisper sweet nothings to her again.

To feel what it might be like to fall for a millionaire cowboy.

Chapter Five

Cabin five was located on a swell of grassland right above the empty main lodge. Everyone who lived around Wycliffe knew the history of Oakvale Ranch: How it'd housed "dudes" during the hard times, how the "city slickers" had kept the Rhodes finances solid.

After the family had struck oil, the dude ranch business had closed, much to the Rhodes's relief. It was no secret that they had barely tolerated the guest operation.

But the legacy still remained, abandoned, silent.

Under a canopy of falling darkness, Emmy paused in front of cabin five's slightly opened door, taking a deep breath. A brandied light stole out of the crack, beckoning to her. She could even catch the aroma of the meal she'd prepared. The inviting weight of saffron loaned her comfort and confidence.

Moving closer, she balanced her fingers on the pine door, pushing it open, promising herself she'd enjoy the supper and...

Don't think about the rest of what he's expecting if you walk inside.

The door opened to reveal a cabin redolent with the scent of lemon polish. Pine-wood furnishings flickered under the light of small candles perched on wrought-iron stands. A fresh Aztec-patterned comforter sprawled over the king-sized bed. In the room's center, she found a hearty dining table, creaking under the weight of her food.

"You're on time tonight," said a low voice from the shaded corner.

Emmy turned to see Deston step into the light, dressed in a black tuxedo and silk shirt. He'd tamed his hair from its usual spiky shambles, but he still wore dark cowboy boots with his evening clothes.

Fingering her own relatively simple dress—a debutante-like frock she'd worn to her culinary school graduation festivities—Emmy felt every inch the inferior. But according to Felicia and Carlota, Lila wasn't flashy anyway; she was a philanthropist, a demure woman who'd spent most of her time reading books in the Oakvale library.

Encouraged by the thought, Emmy stood as tall as

her short stature would allow and smiled with certainty. "I didn't want to embarrass you by not showing. Evidently, your cabin clean-up hasn't gone unnoticed on the ranch, or so my sources tell me."

His eyes, green as the ink on a thousand-dollar bill, glowed in contrast to his tanned skin as he moved toward Emmy. He gestured toward the corner behind her, and the soft strums of an acoustic guitar filled the warm air.

Even though she wanted to look, she couldn't tear her eyes away from Deston. Not yet.

"I should've known someone would see the fuss out here this morning," he said. "I told some of the help that this is about business, but my father bought a cock-and-bull story about me wanting to renovate some of these cabins for my living quarters during those 'future visits' from New York. My parents would do anything to have me on the ranch again, but they know I won't ever move into the big house like J.R. and Bobby from *Dallas*."

Finally overcome by curiosity, Emmy peered over her shoulder at the musician, hoping he wasn't anyone she knew from the staff. But the dark-haired stranger didn't even glance up at her.

Turning back to Deston, she indicated the man, cocking her brow in question.

He grinned, walked to the table and pulled out her chair. "He's from out of town, discreet, and I know you appreciate that."

Warily, with her pulse twanging the veins in her throat, Emmy took her seat. "So if I said, 'Hey, Mr. Music Man,' he'd…?"

The musician kept playing a muted flamenco tune, oblivious.

"He'd ignore you."

Wow. The incredible lives of the rich. No one could touch them if they paid enough for the privilege.

And she was among their crowd right now, wasn't she?

If Deston knew Emmy was a servant, would they be able to talk so easily? Would he be as polite and attentive?

He took the seat across from her, appreciative gaze never wavering. "I'm glad you're here."

Emmy heated up, grinned. "Me, too."

What should she say now? I, Lila Stanhope, came all the way back here just to see you again?

But that would be another woman talking.

She wanted so badly to just be Emmylou tonight.

As he served the chardonnay, then filled her plate with her own scalloped tomatoes with pearl onions, the risotto and chicken Marsala, Emmy watched how he moved. Thought of how every aggressive, smooth gesture would feel if it played out over her body.

A half glass of wine had warmed her to the point where she was longing for his hands to be on her.

But did she have the guts to enjoy what Deston was offering? A no-worries night of pure enjoyment?

Again, Paolo mocked her with his misty promises.

No, she was in control here. Who would ever know about this liaison? It wouldn't be an entire village—that was for certain. It wouldn't be her family, either.

Absently, Emmy touched the locket that hung from an inexpensive chain around her neck.

Deston laid down his fork, leaned over the small table toward her. "I noticed that you wear your heart on the outside."

The soft guitar music lulled her into a relaxed, seductive groove. "It's from my dad." Nigel Brown, Edward Rhodes the Third's former "man."

"I didn't realize your father was so sentimental. He seems more like a diamond or sapphire fan."

He was talking about Mr. Stanhope.

A wave of embarrassment consumed her, another moment of feeling lower than the estate's rich kids.

But Emmy erased those feelings. Even though her father hadn't spent much money on the trinket, it was priceless.

"When he bought this," Emmy said, rubbing her thumb against the tarnished gold, "he opened it up and kissed the inside, where the picture should've gone. That way I could carry him with me."

Carry his love.

Deston's jaw clenched, and he glanced away. "It's good to have a family that close."

Even Lila might have been privy to the proper, stiff lives of the Rhodes clan, but Emmy didn't comment.

The light had gone out of Deston's eyes, so she set down her own utensils and reached across the table to clasp his hand in hers, to summon back the carefree Deston Rhodes.

His skin burned: electric, soothing.

"Let's talk about something fun," she said.

"Name a topic." He squeezed her hand, slightly cheered.

What was safe? "All right. We can share things about ourselves that no one else knows. Silly things, like how, when I bake chocolate chip cookies, I always eat the dough until I get a stomachache."

Generic enough. But it got a smile out of him.

"And you?" she asked.

He paused, wrapping his other hand around hers, enveloping it. "I can't sit in my office chair for more than five minutes at a time. The rest of the day, I pace. I can't stay still when there's work to do."

"I wouldn't be able to sit still, either, if I had a window view of San Antonio. I love the Mexican Market."

"I've got a favorite restaurant there. La Margarita. Great oysters."

Whenever Emmy got to talk food, she couldn't help getting excited. Without thinking, she blurted, "There's this gourmet shop in the Farmer's Market that keeps me occupied for hours. I'm there every Tuesday afternoon, haunting the place."

Her runaway tongue was about to add that she did her weekly wine shopping at the Market, too, because she'd put herself in charge of pairing the wines with the meals, but she stopped cold.

Ooops.

If he noticed that she'd offered a gap in the fortress of her facade, an opportunity to see her if he looked hard enough, he didn't show it. He seemed too distracted.

He'd focused his gaze on her palm, turning it face up, running a hand over the tender inside of her arm. "What else does no one else know about you?"

Emmy quivered. The goosebumps were already taking over. So was relief at having him miss her ill-advised market comment. "Hmmm. My first true love was Ross from *Friends*."

She'd expected him to laugh and ask, "Ross the geek? Not Chandler or Joey?" Instead, a shadow twisted in his eyes.

"Deston?"

"Let's change the subject."

Had she hit a sore spot with the first-love talk? And here she'd thought she was making him happier.

He'd slipped his hand down her arm, fingers lingering on her palm, tracing the center of it. "Maybe we'll look at the future, not the past."

She almost blurted out something about Carlota and her psychic skills, but she bit her tongue instead. Wealthy "Sunny" wouldn't know Carlota the maid.

"What do you see?" she asked, playing along.

She needed to watch herself.

He traced a nail over her love line, spreading tingles from her hand, down her arm, right to the core of her. As he drew light circles, a wave of repressed hunger washed over her, and she bit her lip, keeping it inside.

"I see a man from your past."

His voice was low, a leash drawing her closer.

Using a thumb to tickle her wrist, Deston grinned up at her from underneath a quirked brow.

Devilish, sinful.

When he put just the right amount of pressure on the right nerve, Emmy bolted to the edge of her chair, excitement tweaking her belly.

"Let's forget the rest of dinner," he said.

"I should go. Now," she choked.

"Don't."

The word was bare, crackling with need. Emmy knew she couldn't leave—even if she wanted to.

"Diego," Deston said, rising from his seat, still watching her.

The guitar player stood, head down, as Deston settled payment with him. In the meantime, Emmy also got to her feet, riddled with nerves and sweet tension, shaking with anticipation.

The musician started toward the door, but Deston stopped him with a "Thank you." Nodding, the man finally looked up at Emmy, dark eyes twinkling, then headed out, shutting the door behind him.

The lack of song was deafening, leaving only the

stir of crickets and a still night. Emmy's heartbeat bounced against the walls, throbbing in her ears.

Deston turned around, gaze hungry for her.

Before she knew it, he was across the room, scooping her into his embrace, backing her against a planked wall and cushioning her spine with the bulk of his arms.

He devoured her, his kisses more desperate than last night's, his caresses more urgent.

She felt lost, found, both, as she matched him in passion, grasping his shoulders and dragging him against her.

Emmy was another woman altogether. One she hadn't known existed.

With every thrust of the tongue, he pressed forward, pushing one of her knees to the side, allowing her to feel the extent of his arousal.

She fervently tugged off his jacket, tossed it who-knows-where. Then she ran her hands over his back, kneading, tearing at his shirt to get rid of that, too.

Deston shrugged out of the material, air bathing his naked torso, drying the fine sheen of sweat gathering over his skin.

In his gut, he'd known Sunny would be back for more. He'd seen it in the way she'd glanced over her shoulder at him last night, in the way she hadn't broken that thin thread of yearning that bonded them together.

He hadn't felt such a connection in years. Didn't really want to feel it, because it made sex so much more complicated.

But when he'd seen her pushing open the cabin door, everything else had ceased to exist.

There was only Sunny and his inexplicable need for her.

Quivering candlelight played over her smooth, tanned skin. Panting, she started to undo the front of her tight sundress. She fumbled with the top button, hands shaking.

His breath was also choppy. "Here." His fingers tangled with hers as they fought to get the bodice undone. She abandoned the effort, instead shucking off her intricate sandals, watching him with a mixture of hunger and something much softer in her eyes.

He didn't want to think about what it could turn into if they allowed it to develop.

After he'd taken care of the buttons, he peeled open the material to expose breasts he'd only fantasized about. Small and firm with dusky centers that tightened under his gaze.

Blood pulsating, Deston coaxed his fingers under one of those stimulated mounds, skimming his thumb around her nipple.

Sunny closed her eyes, bit her lip. Made a tiny, pleased sound.

That did it for Deston. He trailed his other hand over her other breast, slowly exploring them.

"Gorgeous," he whispered.

Leaning her head against the wall, she watched him through the thick fringes of her eyelashes, her fingers resting on his wrists, riding each of his gentle strokes.

With a groan, he scooped a hand behind her rear end, cradling her against the wall, bending so he could take a breast into his mouth. He suckled it, ran his tongue around the peak of it until she buried her fingers in his hair and said his name.

"Deston." A fractured whisper.

The sound roared around his head, blocking his sight, his hearing. Funny how he'd already been inside her soul, and he'd escaped through that one heated word.

But you can bet he was going to be inside again.

He laved the other breast, then hesitated, pulling back. Consumed by a burst of momentary happiness, he laughed, then easily lifted her above him using both hands.

She braced herself on his arms, gazing down on him, her short auburn hair winging over her cheeks, her brown eyes wide with passion.

Slowly, he slid her down the front of his body, burying his nose in her modest cleavage, breathing in the scent of her: peaches dripping in whipped cream and honey.

She positioned her legs on either side of him and held his head against her chest, breathing heavily, toying with his dampened hair, then wrapping a leg around his waist.

With infinite care, he turned around, laid her on the bed. She sank into the new comforter, hair spreading like short rays of sienna-tinged sunshine.

In one fluid motion, he glided her dress off, throwing it on a bedside chair. She was left naked except for a pair of butterfly undies.

Surprisingly, his chest fluttered at the sight of them.

He must have stared a beat too long, because she shyly covered her chest with her arms.

"I can't believe this is happening," she said, closing her eyes.

"Believe it." He stilled his heart, telling himself that butterfly panties made no difference in his world. Tender details had no place there.

He leaned on the bed, the mattress dipping as he put his full weight on it, coming to hover over her. With one hand, he removed her arm and exposed a beaded nipple.

She gasped, but allowed him to rest her hand on the bed while he swept his knuckles over the curve of her breast.

"You've got a little mole right here." He bent to kiss the perfect mark on the side.

She moved with his mouth, reaching for him.

"Deston?"

"Mmm?" He licked her skin, from nipple to collarbone, lightly biting her neck.

In response, she circled his body with her legs, plucked at the waistband of his pants. "When I was young, I never thought we'd…"

She bit her lower lip as he trailed a hand over her stomach, to her underwear. Through the cotton, he nuzzled an index finger between her folds, rubbing until she wiggled her hips.

"We'd what, darlin'?"

She grabbed his hand and guided him into her panties. "This."

He chuckled and brought her to further readiness, coasting a finger inside her, swirling it around, using his thumb to add to her restlessness.

Rocking against his hand, she grabbed a handful of comforter. "I want more."

"How do you know there's more?" Watching her strain and flush fascinated him.

With a frustrated mewl, she cupped him.

"There's more," she said, *oooh*ing as he used his thumb to put a little more pressure on her slick center.

Driven by her sexy sound, he captured her lips with his, taking his time with a lazy, teasing kiss.

"More?" he asked.

She started undoing his belt, and Deston laughed.

As he rose from the bed, she unabashedly watched.

When he grinned at her, she glanced away. Her fingers touched the locket around her neck, and she unclasped it, tucking it behind an antique water pitcher and bowl on the nightstand.

Obviously, the necklace held great emotional attachment, something Deston had weaned himself off years ago.

Banishing the memories, he reached into a pocket, then dropped a condom on the bed. Their gazes met, and Sunny blew out a long breath, sitting up and moving backward to the pillows. There she rested, chin on folded knees.

Damn, she looked tumbled. Warmed-up, bedheaded and primed for more.

Deston had suspected Sunny would be a kitten with him—after all, she'd been just as playful at the swimming hole—but he hadn't expected the fiery way she matched him. Or the sudden shyness.

He discarded his boots and pants, finding Sunny's gaze bathing him in soft adoration.

Caution flashed over his sight, a yellow glare of warning.

But his body would have none of the wariness.

It hammered with the insistent thrash of lust traveling his limbs. As he came back to Sunny, his pulse picked up speed.

He wrapped her against him again, starting with a kiss—one that revved and roared with growing impatience. By this time, he was aroused to the point of explosion.

Both of them slipped off her underwear, and there she was. Vulnerable.

His.

He took a moment to appreciate her with a drawn-out glance, but she pulled him to her, covering her body with his.

"Wait." He juggled the condom.

This time, she took over. "Here."

With trembling fingers, she opened the packet, then slid the rubber over his length.

"Here's to New York," she whispered.

He couldn't utter a word.

While Sunny leaned back on the pillows, she pulled him down, then led him inside.

He'd held back so long that he wasn't sure he'd be able to help himself. But if there was one thing Deston practiced, it was control.

He glided into her, and she soared with him, absorbing every easy thrust. Her muscles embraced him, warmed him with the eroticism of slippery comfort.

They moved together, and the night's symphony overwhelmed him, singeing him with the familiar cadence of joined bodies. Every bead of sweat dropping from his chest to hers was a note of lost music. Every moan was a harmonious chord that wafted into the air, spent.

Finally, she cried out, an ultimate release. As her aria veiled him, he sought his own satisfaction, driving into her until the pillows fell to the ground from her thrashing. She arched up to him, urging him on, and, in that crazy moment, all he wanted was for her to feel more for him than anyone else ever had.

Finally, he climaxed, shuddered, out of breath and energy, his heart sounding tinny and small, chased by something much bigger.

While their sweat mingled, he held her, stroking her hair as their breathing evened out.

"I never thought it'd be this way between us, either," he said in an unguarded moment, the words escaping him before he could help it.

One of the candles sizzled to darkness, and Deston looked over to see that most of them had burned out.

Sunny stirred, then got to her elbow to gaze at him. Her eyes were shiny, filled with an emotion Deston didn't want to name.

He'd seen it too many times before, after a light night of lovemaking.

Maybe, this time, he even felt something inside of himself weakening.

As he adjusted to her new position, he slid out of her.

They both froze when they saw that the condom had broken.

At first, Emmy wasn't sure what had happened. She was only aware of an excess of moisture between her thighs, something she'd never felt with Paolo.

Deston muttered a harsh curse.

"Did it…?"

"Yeah." He glanced at her from beneath lowered brows, then cursed again.

Oh, no. She knew she'd pay a price for lying to him. Bad acts always came back to you, didn't they? That's why she'd tried to be a decent person during most of her life.

Until now, when she'd given into one night of longing.

He used the bed sheet to wipe the wetness from between her thighs, silent.

"I'm sorry, Deston. I—I don't know why I'm apologizing, but—"

"This isn't your fault."

"I'm not on the pill." There'd been just one man in her life, and this was the only chance she'd taken since.

With brooding intensity, he finished cleaning her off.

"What if…?" she asked.

He tossed the sheet aside. "Damn it all."

There were a lot of questions to be asked: What would they do if she got pregnant? Was live-for-now Deston even ready to be a father?

Was she ready to be a mother?

Her heart gave an extra-nervous hop. "Maybe it's nothing to worry about."

"I am worried, Sunny. I'm always so careful about this. It's never happened before."

He stood, retrieving his pants, pulling them on again.

Another candle lost its battle to stay alight. Then another. But there was still enough illumination to bask over his wide shoulders, the muscled arms, the granite-cut abs, the tapered waist and hips.

Emmy's heart swelled with an emotion that had bloomed during their lovemaking. She couldn't help it. He'd brought out the sleeping urge to feel loved, even for a few hours of false hope.

But she knew the deal—and getting pregnant wasn't a part of it.

He turned to her again. "If you should…" He motioned with his hands.

"Find myself carrying a baby?"

"That." He ran a hand through his brown hair.

No doubt about it. He wasn't ready for kids.

Especially with the estate's cook.

She couldn't saddle him with that stigma by asking him for a promise to do right by her. Marrying another rich person like Lila Stanhope would be one thing for Deston. He'd become his father and live like a true Rhodes in a marriage that was more business than love.

But marrying Emmylou Brown?

Wouldn't happen. Edward Rhodes the Third would never allow her past the threshold, and that was a fact based on Harry Rhodes's experience.

Emmy couldn't even stand the thought of having Deston provide for a baby without marriage. It'd be too much like what Paolo had intended for her—to be a mistress instead of a respectable wife.

She'd never settle for that.

Besides, maybe this was God's way of putting a good scare in her, to override her hormones and bat some sense into her brain.

Misleading him had been wrong, and the game had

to end here. If she could just return to her cottage and clean up, she would stay away from him for good.

She had to.

Deston was heading toward the bathroom. "I'll get a washcloth."

Emmy slipped out of bed while he used a struggling candle for light and scrounged around the cabinets. Quickly, she dressed, catching sight of Deston in the bathroom mirror.

He was combing his fingers through his hair again, clearly frustrated and angry. Disappointment melted through her.

She was good enough to have sex with, but not to keep. Message received loud and clear. After all, this was the second time she'd gotten it.

Once in the Tuscan region, once now.

With one last, heartfelt glance, she padded toward the door and took wing, putting an end to his suffering.

A few minutes later, Deston said, "I don't think I can get water." He hadn't hooked up electricity or other utilities, thinking this would be the only night he'd use the cabin. He wouldn't need it on the east coast.

He came out of the bathroom, dry washcloth in hand.

Empty.

"Sunny?"

While he looked around, he dropped the terry cloth, heart frantically beating.

He raised his voice. "Sunny!"

Her clothes were gone. Another candle gave up its light, leaving only a few to guide him. He opened the door, but found only a slight wind creeping along the grass, rustling the oak leaves.

He whooshed the door shut, dousing all but one candle.

A helpless quaking claimed him, taking over his limbs, seeking shelter in the pit of his belly.

He remembered another night, when the ambulance had pulled away from the fraternity house with Juliet in it. He'd seen her, covered to the neck with a blanket, face pale, blazing red hair matted and clinging to her head.

Sirens blazing, they'd driven away, leaving Deston to rage and wonder what had happened to the woman who said she'd try to fit in with his family, the woman he'd brought home to his parents so they could meet his future wife.

Juliet Templeton.

She'd lied to him about who she really was: a girl with the proper pedigree, but with the wrong appetites. She'd lied about being with other men. She'd lied about the lowbrow parties his parents would've hated.

She'd taken away almost every ounce of trust Deston had been born with.

Now, Sunny had run away with what little had been left.

He had to get her back, just to see if she was going to have his child. God knew what he'd do after that, but Deston Rhodes never left a situation flapping in the wind. If he had to get married, Sunny was the best option—a society woman who had the Rhodes stamp of approval.

Still stifling the attack of his conscience, Deston sank down to the mattress, burying his face in his hands. Through his fingers, he saw a glimmer of something golden on the nightstand, behind the pitcher and bowl.

He reached out for it, cupping Sunny's locket in his palm.

The last candle died out, leaving Deston in the dark.

Chapter Six

"I'll take you to the doctor," Carlota said, holding out her palms in supplication as she sat on the bed in Emmy's cottage.

Emmy shook her head. "It's been only five days since I was with Deston, so I don't see the hurry. And another conversation about this won't change my mind."

Truthfully, she was putting off fretting about it until she got her period…or didn't.

Emmy wanted more time to figure out what to do about her wild night with the man of her dreams—if she needed to do anything at all.

Felicia leaned forward on a red futon Emmy had

found at the Salvation Army store. "You can't live in denial, Em. What if you're—"

"Please don't say it."

Her friend's eyes went sad, and Emmy sat next to her. "I know how you feel, Felicia. If you were the one with pregnancy possibilities, we'd be dancing on the lawn. But…"

She didn't have to finish. Emmy's circumstances really could've been better. She could be having the baby of someone who loved her and wanted to marry her.

But that wasn't the case.

In order to ease Deston's mind, Emmy had written him a short note, thanking him for the dinner, reassuring him that everything would turn out fine. She'd mailed it during an unplanned trip to San Antonio the next day, hoping he'd stay true to his no-strings-attached philosophy and the arrogant attitude she'd come to expect of wealthy people. Hoping he'd forget about the night with Sunny and any ensuing responsibilities.

She knew she was being naive, but contacting him again was out of the question, no matter the outcome.

Felicia sniffed, then lifted her chin, positive as ever in the face of her troubles. Sometimes Emmy wondered if anything ever got to Felicia, but she knew the irony of this situation definitely did, no matter how her friend smiled through it.

Funny how Felicia would give her life to have a

baby, and Emmy was the one who might accidentally have a child.

"Let's talk about you," Felicia said on an upbeat note, moisture welling in her eyes, "not about my issues."

The blonde wiped away a stray tear, but Emmy didn't let go of her. Right now, her friends were more of an anchor than anyone else. She couldn't tell her mom—not until she knew the result of a pregnancy test.

Even thinking about Francesca Brown's reaction made Emmy a little nervous. When Mama found out that her daughter had been with Deston Rhodes and had fooled him in the process, she'd get that disappointed look on her face—the one Emmy had imagined over the telephone line after she'd revealed her tryst with Paolo in Francesca's home village of Tocchi.

The friends sat in thoughtful silence until Emmy broke it.

"He's going to New York tomorrow."

They all knew who "he" was. Carlota and Felicia, both still dressed in their black-and-white maid's uniforms since they were merely on lunch hour, fixed their gazes on her.

"We knew the day would come," Carlota said, resting her chin on a hand. "We were banking on it."

"I should be relieved." Emmy took her arm away from Felicia's shoulders. "No more wearing those baggy clothes. No more listening for his voice so I can hide from him."

"It's a good thing he's leaving," Felicia said.

Without thinking, Emmy's hand crept to her belly, resting over the still-flat plane of it.

Hey, little guy or girl, she thought. Are you in there? Maybe no one's home. Or maybe you're just waiting to come out some day. And if you are, I'll try to make this such a wonderful world for you. A world where you don't answer "Yes, Sir" or work someone else's schedule.

Is anyone there?

Feeling foolish, Emmy allowed her hand to drift up to her neck, where her locket should've been. She knew she'd left it in the dude cabin. It was like losing a piece of herself. Carlota had volunteered to sneak back and search for it, under the readied pretense of "Lila Stanhope" having called the house in the hopes of finding it.

But Carlota had had no luck.

"Life would be much simpler if I could've stayed in that cabin with him for the rest of our lives," Emmy said, hand dropping to the futon. "Not that he would've been happy with the surroundings."

Carlota laughed without amusement. "You're right. No upstairs person would be caught dead living in a cabin. That's Deston's appeal though, isn't it? The ultra-rich playboy who can sweep you off your feet?"

Sure, the fantasy still held her in thrall. It always would. But she'd met Deston on a more personal level, too. She had seen sadness shade the planes of his chiseled jaw and cheekbones. She had seen a side she hadn't known existed.

A tender side. A side that could make a great father someday.

Again, she rested a hand on her stomach. It was becoming a habit, a great comfort.

Hey, you.

Felicia noticed the gesture, and she placed a slim palm over it. Carlota wandered over, also, joining the could-be family.

"When do you think he or she will realize we're out here?" Felicia asked.

Emmy's pulse popped. Excitement or fear? "I'm not sure. I'll look it up in a baby book."

"A doctor might be able to tell you," Carlota said.

Felicia gasped. "I felt something!"

"That's because I haven't had lunch, silly." Emmy lightly squeezed Felicia's and Carlota's hands in hers.

"No matter what happens," Carlota said, dark-brown eyes wide, "we'll be here, Em."

"We'll all raise the baby together." Felicia laughed. "He or she will have three mothers."

"And a happy grandmother, to boot." Even though Emmy dreaded revealing her pregnancy, she knew her mama would love and treasure the baby.

Just as Emmy would.

The epiphany took her aback: a little boy or girl. Hers and Deston's.

She couldn't help smiling.

Carlota stood, then pressed her fingers to her temple. She wandered over to the bed, where she sat, head in hands.

Felicia and Emmy glanced at each other. When Carlota got a headache, that meant one of two things: She was going to suffer for a few hours, or she was getting a vision.

"Car?" Felicia asked.

"I'm okay."

Emmy got up to fetch aspirin, just in case.

On her way out of the rest room, Emmy heard Carlota's matter-of-fact words: "He's going to stay in Texas and look for her."

The medicine bottle thunked to the carpet, the pills rattling against the plastic. She thought about her in-the-moment confession of going to the Mexican Market every Tuesday.

Carlota rubbed her forehead, then sat up straight, lost in thought.

"Carlota?" Felicia asked. "Anything more?"

They never doubted their friend's predictions. Carlota's psychic and empathetic abilities had been a part of their lives since they were children growing up on Oakvale. All she had to do was touch someone to feel their futures, not that a vision came every time there was contact. Still, Carlota was careful to keep to herself much of the time.

Emmy couldn't imagine reading other people's

thoughts and futures, how that could affect your life, your confidence.

Carlota paused, then gave Emmy an understanding look. "Deston's not going to New York. At least not now. It looks like you're going to be wearing Felicia's weird outfits for the next millennium."

"Are you getting feelings about a baby?" Felicia asked eagerly.

Carlota shook her head. "No."

A keening ache traveled Emmy's chest. "No baby then?"

"That doesn't mean you're not pregnant," Carlota said. "Still, aren't you relieved?"

"I'm not sure." The tightness wrapped around her heart, squeezing. "No. I'm...I'm mixed up."

"He's got to be in love with you if he's searching," Felicia said, perking up.

Emmy curtailed her hope. "Let's not jump to conclusions. Maybe he's being honorable in finding me and making sure he doesn't have a child to raise."

Neither Carlota nor Felicia said anything.

"I'm not going to get whiplashed by a man again, you-all. I'm not going to think there's more to Deston staying than it appears."

"Want me to help you dress for the garden, just in case he hasn't gotten tired of visiting with the servants?" Felicia asked.

The "beekeeper" suit. It was bunched at the bottom of her closet because Emmy had thought she wouldn't need it after today's vegetable gathering. Not unless Deston visited in the future, which, from the way he talked, sounded unlikely.

"What a tangled web," Carlota said.

Emmy agreed, very much feeling caught up in her own silken dreams.

Whenever Deston needed to clear his mind in San Antonio, he hit the state-of-the-art gym in the office. But here at Oakvale, he had the luxury of riding the range.

Even though visits back to the family ranch were usually more stressful than enjoyable, he didn't want to leave. Not now.

As the afternoon sun blazed overhead, he guided his horse, Mouse, through former cattle pasture, now abandoned to thickets of grapevine, switchgrass and mealy sage. Man and beast cut through the juniper-leaf-scented air to the dude cabins.

He was drawn back here like spring water flowing downhill.

Using slight pressure on the reins, Deston signaled Mouse to pause. The horse stamped his feet, nickering, probably feeling his master's agitation.

The cabin. Since that night, Deston had hired the cleaning crew to clear it out again, causing his dad to ask what in tarnation was going on out here. Deston didn't deign to respond, but that wasn't unusual.

Only one question concerned him: Where had Sunny gone?

Through the cabin's time-faded windows, he caught a memory of candlelight, of their bare bodies intertwined on the bed, of her beautiful face glowing with the flush of a higher emotion.

Deston tore his gaze away and turned Mouse back to the ranch.

As he rode, escorted by the twitter of warblers, he reached into his shirt pocket, where he kept the necklace.

Taking it out, he saw how the sun reflected off the pendant's gold casing, the brightness reminding him of Sunny's smile.

Unwelcome feelings reached into his chest and tugged.

With a frown, Deston put the locket away again. Sunny had left no way to contact her, but that had been the appeal of their affair. Even though he'd received a polite, removed thank-you note postmarked in San Antonio, Deston wasn't sure where to start his search—if he decided to embark on one.

Should he contact Elijah Stanhope with the excuse that housekeeping had found his daughter's locket in her guest room?

Dammit, he needed to get a hold of himself. After Juliet had died, Deston had made a vow never to go through such self-doubt and agony again. And he'd been fine with his uneventful affairs before now.

So why was this any different?

Because Sunny makes you feel more powerless

than ever, he thought. She'd stirred up more than just a physical need to spend the night with a woman.

Dammit, her inaccessibility ate at him.

You'd think the locket would've lured her back. Had he mistaken her tenderheartedness for something more? Or had she been playing the seduction game as well as he had?

No. Not Sunny.

Maybe, if she didn't contact him in a few weeks, he'd get in touch with a P.I. to discreetly find her, just to reassure himself that all was normal. If she wasn't pregnant, then he could arrange to have her locket sent by mail and that would be that. His responsibility to her would be ended.

Unless...

Deston found it hard to swallow. A father. Him.

What a joke.

If life had any sense of justice, it would see that Sunny wasn't carrying his child. Because by the time Deston found out for certain, he'd surely be over this fascination for her.

Then he could go back to his old, carefree life.

By this time, he'd arrived back at the stables. After brushing down Mouse, he made his way to the big house, intending to return to San Antonio tonight so he could oversee final preparations for tomorrow's move to New York. His assistants in the city had been taking care of the finer details, so he was just about set.

But not entirely willing to leave.

As he walked up the rise toward the big house, the vegetable gardens caught his eye. They were located near the stone cottages, Francesca Brown's in particular. But she'd recently moved to a smaller cottage on the grounds, a "retirement" boon that the Rhodes family offered employees who still had relatives on the estate. The older cook had given hers up for the daughter, Emmylou, in anticipation of assuming her new post and letting the younger woman have a place of her own.

He'd learned a lot about the servants in these last few days, making up for the guilt of never acknowledging them in the past. When Edward Rhodes had caught wind of Deston's crusade to learn names, he had scolded him over dinner.

But Deston hadn't heard a word.

As he neared the mansion, a flash of white stirred behind the tomato plants, halting him.

Was that Emmylou Brown? The girl temporarily without a voice?

Her clothing engulfed her body, stealing her shape. He couldn't tell how tall she was or what color her hair was, but Deston supposed she resembled her mom and Nigel Brown.

God, he missed the butler—his dry sense of humor, his wink whenever he'd catch Deston slipping out the back door so he could run free over the lawns.

In spite of Deston's quiet attachment to Emmylou's dad, she clearly had no interest in him. Like a lot of the servants, except for her blond friend, the maid Felicia, she'd been pretty aloof when he'd introduced himself. But that was fine. Not everyone had warmth.

Warmth like Sunny's—a smile that made you feel right at home.

His body reacted to the memory of his lover's breasts, tiny waist, flat stomach, slender legs.

The trill of a cell phone jerked him back to the reality of standing on a hill, watching the cook's daughter brush dirt from a potato.

Potato. Food.

Another memory from that night jerked at his conscience, and he grabbed onto it.

Tuesdays. Mexican Market.

Hadn't Sunny said she went there every week? True, he hadn't been listening all that well, but…

Did he have the guts to risk finding her there?

Heart pounding with the possibilities, he unclipped the ringing phone from his belt, accessed it. "Rhodes here."

It was his trusted assistant from the San Antonio office, wondering when Deston was coming back. "I found something in the books you'd be interested in seeing," Elaine said.

He'd assigned her to investigate his worst fears— that his father was paying Stanhope employees to sabotage their employer's holdings, thus degrading the value of the business and making it easy for Rhodes

Industries to underbid in their quest to own Stanhope Steel.

"I'm on my way," he said. "Thanks, Elaine."

He ended the call and attached the phone to his belt again. Dammit, he hoped his father wasn't dealing from the bottom of the deck.

Not only did the underhanded tactics go against Deston's nature, but this was the Stanhopes they were dealing with. Lila.

Sunny.

Strangely, he felt a little protective of her, inexplicably possessive.

Deston wouldn't see the Stanhopes get ruined by his family.

Pride and *Texas*—words he'd been raised on.

So where was his father's pride?

Driven by righteous anger and thankful for something to take his mind off Sunny, Deston strode toward the big house, intending to settle back in San Antonio as soon as possible.

New York could wait.

From the gardens, Emmy watched him stalk up the hill, emotions burning in her throat.

Even through the darkness of her sunglasses, she could detect subtle nuances about him—how the angle of his cowboy hat hid his handsome face, how his aggressive walk could be reflecting an anger which would tighten his mouth and harden his eyes.

Did he ever think about the other night?

Ridiculous. She was the one with all the schoolgirl fantasies. Deston had probably moved on to other women by now, and she couldn't complain about it.

His nature was well-known. She'd accepted it for what it was worth.

And she'd deal with the consequences if need be.

She lay down a potato and positioned her hands over her lower stomach, smiling.

"That's him. Your dad. Not that you can tell, but he's a handsome devil. You know, I think you'll have a lighter shade of brown hair, just like your dignified grandpapa. And I hope you'll have your dad's green eyes."

Emmy glanced up again, watching as Deston disappeared through the back door. She knew it led to a mud room, where he'd kick the dirt off his boots and deposit his Stetson, since Leticia Rhodes didn't allow hats to be worn inside the main house.

"Where do you think he's going in such a huff?"

Like a dolt, she waited for an answer, realizing that there might not be anyone inside to respond.

Her palms fell away from her belly as she held back the sadness, held back the fervent urge to enter the big house through the upstairs door, to tell Deston she was right here.

A world away.

Chapter Seven

Several days later, Deston's world turned upside down.

Still reeling from a phone call he'd received earlier in the day, he wandered away from La Margarita Mexican Restaurant and Oyster Bar in San Antonio's Mexican Market. Even though Deston had been distracted by the call, he'd fulfilled a promise to meet a client here for lunch. He always brought out-of-town associates to the Mexican Market for the myriad shops and regional color, for the mariachis, rainbow-skirted dancers and historical charm.

At least, that was his excuse on this Tuesday.

Before today's phone call, he'd planned to wander

by that gourmet shop just to see if Sunny was there. She hadn't specified a time other than "afternoon" for her weekly shopping trip, but he'd been willing to take the chance.

Yet this morning, before the call, life had been less chaotic. Now, he was still assimilating the details of the mysterious message he'd received.

He sank to a wooden bench, disgusted by his very association with Rhodes Industries. Tourists and locals bustled by him as they sought deals from the stores and stalls, but Deston didn't fully register the activity.

I won't tell you my name, the voice on the end of the line had said, *but I'm not the only one who's been paid to loosen a few factory screws here and there. I hate what's happening, but I needed the cash.*

The man had said he was calling from a public phone, but Deston would use an investigative agency to track down the location, even though the odds were against him finding anything.

Fruitless. Yet he needed to do *something.*

For the past few days, he'd lived at the San Antonio offices, steering clear of his crate-filled condo in favor of working with Elaine, the assistant who'd more or less adopted him over their years together. The older woman had been hired by Deston when he'd first become a CEO, and she was loyal to him until the end.

That's why he trusted her to help investigate, to communicate with his father, creating excuses for Deston to still be in San Antonio rather than New York.

His oyster lunch sat heavily in his stomach as his phone rang.

"Rhodes here."

Elaine's low, scratchy voice assaulted him with words that didn't quite fit together at first. "Our P.I. firm is well worth the bucks we pay them, kid. Not only have they already tracked our phone caller—I don't know how hard he was trying to hide, truth to tell—but they gathered from our source that the pay-offs are originating from the Caymans."

Why not? Wasn't that a popular spot for criminals to do their business? "So my father's got to have someone there who's doling out the money."

"What's our next step then?"

It took a moment for all the news to converge into a big picture.

Payoffs. Sabotage. The Stanhopes and other business owners the Rhodes had worked over in the past.

Sunny.

If their futures were as entwined as those fortune-telling grooves on her palms, how could he face her again, knowing his family was out to get hers?

Finally, Deston answered. "Looks like I won't be going to New York any time soon, but Charles Nickerson can take care of matters there." Nickerson was Deston's right-hand man, so he wouldn't worry on that front. "And I'm sure as hell not going back to Oakvale. If I see the old man, I'm likely to tear him apart."

"Don't do that until you're absolutely sure of what's happening."

"Do you think Harry's involved?"

Right now, his brother ran the Los Angeles branch of the company, so Deston couldn't see him having his hand in the same pot as their father's.

Still… "Have the P.I.s turn their attention to that angle, too, would you, Elaine?"

"Will do."

Deston ran a hand over his features, mapping the weary lines settling over skin he'd always thought was so tough. "How the hell can I respect my father now?"

The phone reception crackled. "As I said, get some more proof before you go off the deep end."

Proof.

Deston stood, full of livid steam, and headed down the market plaza. The displays of maracas, piñatas and hand woven blankets all swirled together in his anger.

He wouldn't feel helpless. No damned way. And forget about going back to the office to wait for the P.I.s to call with their findings.

Deston needed to take care of matters. To speed things up so he could confront his father and put an end to the dirty dealings before the Stanhopes caught on.

Hell, why did the Stanhopes matter so much anyway? He wasn't doing this for them. For Lila.

Not at all.

"Elaine, I'm going to see what's going on for myself."

"You're not—"

"You bet I am. I'm going down to the Cayman Islands to track our connection down. Could you make arrangements to ready the private jet? And for accommodations?"

"Deston, if your daddy hears that you've gone there, he'll know something's going on."

Damn. "What if I bring along a P.I. to do the footwork on Grand Cayman, and when he uncovers our man, I'll be nearby, tucked away, ready to roll?"

"Better plan. How about taking some R&R in Miami Beach while you wait?" she asked hopefully.

"You want me to relax?" He stalked past a sign pointing toward the Farmer's Market.

"Lord knows you need it. And you can tell big Mr. Rhodes that this is your last fandango before moving to New York. We'll use more of your private funds to send our P.I. on a charter flight to the Caymans while the jet stands by for you in Miami."

"Elaine, what would I do without your intellect?"

The older woman gave a smoker's low laugh. "Don't forget my beauty, too, kid."

He'd reached the indoor, air-conditioned Farmer's Market by now. Sunny's gourmet store was in there. He knew, because he'd located it before lunch.

As Elaine rattled off questions about resorts, Deston went in, answering every query, and sat on the edge of a bench. He surveyed the crowd, adrenaline pumping through him.

His assistant sighed over the phone. "No wonder Mr. Rhodes wanted you out of this office. There sure are some cow patties hitting the wall down here."

"Elaine?"

"Yes, babydoll?"

Deston hadn't taken his eyes off the shoppers, searching their faces, desperately needing to be grounded in something other than this nightmare. "I won't forget your loyalty."

"I know that. It's not everyone I'd stick out my neck for. Now you get ready to leave, and I'll take care of things on this end."

"Sounds good. I'm calling the P.I. firm. I'd like Hatcher to work this."

"Y'all be careful."

Deston tried to smile. "You watch yourself, too. 'Bye."

He shut the phone, clipped it to his belt. Why was he still lollygagging around here? Sure, it'd be a while before the jet was ready to take off, but he had a million things to do.

A petite woman with short brown hair caught Deston's eye and he jerked to attention. She peeked into the gourmet store's window, then turned around when a man came up from behind to hug her.

She wasn't Sunny.

Deston's stomach dipped to his booted toes.

Ridiculous, to have his mind on her when it should be on business.

But she was part of that business.

Maybe he could make some phone calls while he sat here on this bench. There's no way he was going back to the Rhodes Industries office, not with all the rage his father had stirred up inside Deston. Right now, he didn't want anything to do with his own family.

During the next hour, he got hold of Hatcher and gave the P.I. instructions. He checked in with Elaine to hear that the jet was being readied and she'd booked the penthouse suite at a luxury resort in South Beach, a trendy Miami playground for the terminally hip. A perfect cover. His efficient Woman Friday had also ordered clothing and toiletries that would be awaiting him.

All the while, Deston watched the crowd, waited, holding his breath every time a small-boned, short-haired brunette happened by.

God, he needed to see Sunny. His body cried out for her comforting scent—the one that reminded him of kitchen aromas, of all the sweet ingredients that drew a naughty kid to a pie cooling on a windowsill.

But if she did come, what would he say to her?

Sunny, it's great to see you. By the way, it looks like my family is trying to decimate your business so Rhodes Industries can buy it for a song.

Or would he stay true to his blood just a little longer, betraying her with his silence?

Damn the old man. They'd had their differences in the past, but this was something more dangerous.

Emotionally baffled, desperate for some solace, Deston kept watching the crowd, counting the minutes until he could board the jet and escape.

Since Emmy hadn't seen Deston at the Mexican Market last Tuesday during her weekly shopping trip, she'd convinced herself that he hadn't heard her verbal flub during their dinner conversation.

What a relief. Really.

Now, as she headed through the nippy conditioned air of the Farmer's Market, past the gleam of turquoise-and-silver jewelry and the thick scent of leather-worked goods, she tried to take her mind off Deston yet again.

But it was impossible. She still had a few days before her period was due, and she wasn't going to worry until then.

But she did worry. Every day, as a matter of fact.

And it wasn't doing any good.

As she approached her favorite store, exotic spices and seasonings wafted to her, pulling her inside. Every time she came here, the stock differed, affecting her senses in various ways. Today they turned her stomach a little. Maybe the store had ordered a new product that her nose didn't appreciate.

She had a shopping list, knowing she could buy hard-to-find materials here: spices from Mexico, India and South America, cheeses, vinegars, oils and various cooking toys. With a spring in her step, she went about her business, inspecting jars, dreaming up new recipes, lost in her surroundings.

"Sunny."

At first, she didn't know if Deston's familiar voice was in her head or…

Lungs aching with the breath she was holding, Emmy slowly turned around.

A burst of heat blindsided her.

Yes!

Oh, no.

Butterflies—more like B-52s—divebombed inside her chest. He was more handsome than she recalled, if that was possible. So tall, powerful. His eyes flashed over her, and a slight smile edged his lips.

Was he happy to see her? Because with each passing second, his gaze darkened. Finally, he glanced away.

"I thought it was you," he said, straightening, meeting her gaze again with new strength. He clenched his jaw, withdrawing without even stepping away.

"Deston. I…" What could she say? "I didn't expect to see you again."

"That's what we both wanted, if I remember correctly."

The logical response to that would've been, "So why are you here?" But she already knew. They were past speaking around the could-be pregnancy.

"Did you get my note?" she asked instead.

"The one in which you told me not to fret? Yeah.

But it didn't say anything about why you ran off that night."

That's because she couldn't explain it herself. Not without telling him about Paolo and her real identity.

"I'm a big girl," she said. "I didn't need you to minister to me."

The words hurt, because Emmy would've given her heart to have lingered in his arms, to have been stroked and cared for by him. But she'd seen his anger, the turmoil of a man who didn't want anything long-term.

Her reminder must've gotten to him, because he propped his hands on his hips underneath the swanky business jacket.

"How are you?" he asked.

"Not pregnant." Yet.

Surprisingly, he didn't react. She'd expected him to grab his heart and heft a huge sigh.

"I suppose it's still early."

"Listen," Emmy turned to a rack and absently picked up a package of Ethiopian berbere. "This conversation could go in circles for the next hour. I know you're too busy for that, and so am I."

"Who're you cooking dinner for?"

She cocked an eyebrow at him. "Myself."

And it was true. Cooking made Emmy feel as if she'd conquered a mountain. The skill defined her, convinced her she could reach beyond the downstairs kitchen.

"Is it a hobby?" he asked.

"Deston? What is this?"

He gave an enigmatic shrug. "I guess I'm small-talking with you."

Odd. Their exchanges had always been a means to an end. Seductive conversation. A warm-up to their hot kisses.

Emmy put the berbere back on the rack. "Honestly, you confuse me. First you don't go to New York after all, then you show up here, then you start asking questions… Why?"

He didn't say anything for a moment, merely perused a shelved cluster of Mediterranean marjoram jars.

"Deston?"

"Have you ever been to Miami? South Beach?"

Okay, so he wanted to change the subject. Again. Was there any in-bounds topic with him?

"No. But I've heard of it. Movie stars, playboys… Hardly my speed."

"I'll be traveling there for a few days."

"It's a nice place to vacation, I'm sure." Why did she have to sound so wistful?

Deston reached over, traced her cheekbone. Caught off guard, Emmy captured his hand with hers. He held on to her fingers.

"I've missed you, Sunny. And…I'm sorry."

Sorry? For the condom breaking? Or…?

He was running hot and cold, and Emmy wasn't sure what was going through his mind.

A flare of unidentified emotion intensified his gaze.

"Come with me," he said.

Emmy laughed, shocked. "To South Beach?"

Truthfully, he looked just as shocked to have said it. "Yeah. We'll get away from Oakvale, away from your family. No one will know us if we escape."

Her head began to tumble with "buts."

Her job on the estate. Her mama. Her lies.

He must've sensed her doubts. "Just for a few days. I've got business nearby, but that'll still leave us with some time to ourselves. Some time to indulge."

Emmy was already shaking her head.

"And," he continued, tightening his grasp on her hand, "every luxury will be at your disposal, without expectation."

This was too tempting, being offered a holiday with him, and on a silver platter besides.

"What do you mean," she asked, "without expectation?"

He linked fingers with hers, and the gesture was sweet rather than seductive.

"It means whatever you want it to."

"Wait, none of this makes sense."

"Right." He chuckled a little. "Same here. I think I just want to be around you, Sunny. I've got a penthouse suite reserved. It has more than one bedroom."

"So this isn't anything…sexual? We already had a scare."

He smiled, more to himself than to her. "We'll just be more careful."

Desire shot through her. It was mixed with fear, frustration. "So this *is* about sex."

Another customer walked past them, reducing them to pulse-pounding silence.

She had a chance to bask in the sun, to live a life she'd only dreamed about with a man beyond her reach. All her days, Emmy had been on the outside peeking in, wishing she could smooth the knots from her mama's overworked hands, wishing she could cook romantic meals for two and enjoy them with a man who loved her.

The reasons to refuse him escaped her muddled brain.

He didn't say anything until they were alone again. "I can't lie and say that I don't want you with every screaming hormone in my body. But, at the same time, I think we should…I don't know…talk more."

"Because of the just-in-case factor." Because of their maybe-baby.

"I'm going to do right by you if there's a child."

Something fluttered against the lining of Emmy's belly. She placed her hand there, her throat burning.

He cares about what happens to you.

The realization broke her heart, because she knew he was just going through the motions.

"I can't blame you for wanting to discuss the future," she said, "but…"

"But what?"

But I'm not your socialite, she thought.

He held her hand to his heart. Under the muscles of his chest, she felt a pattering rhythm. He was just as wary of this proposition as she was.

"I want you there more than anything else on this earth, Sunny."

Dang it. How could she say no? Katrina, one of the kitchen assistants, could take Emmy's place for a few days; she'd helped her mama for years. But what could Emmy tell Mama? That she had a once-in-a-lifetime chance to fly away with the boy…the *man* she'd always been half in love with?

"I can't," she said.

"Hey now." He enveloped her in his arms with a mixture of determination and gentleness. "If I have to kidnap you on my private jet, I will."

The breath whooshed out of her as he held her close. "You're not joking, are you?"

"No. And I'm not taking no for an answer." He scooped her into the cradle of his arms and swept her out the door. "Come on."

"This is crazy!" And wonderful.

He was so strong, so sure in his stride. They passed onlookers who stared with amusement, amazement. One man pumped his fist in the air and shouted, "You show her who's boss!"

Out of the corner of her eye, Emmy saw the man's significant other punch him in the arm. Hard.

"A few days," Deston said. "That's all I'm asking of you. And believe me, I'm in no mood to kid around."

"That's obvious. You're really not letting me go?"

"Hell, no. You'll scamper away again."

If she hadn't wanted this to happen, she'd be angry. But she did. Oh, God, she did.

"Can I at least go home to pack? To make a few phone calls and then meet you?"

"They've got clothes and toothbrushes in Florida, too, and you can make calls on my cell phone."

"I can't go," she repeated, panicked.

"You don't have a choice."

A roar of hot air enveloped them as he carried her outside, past the stalls, toward her fantasies.

He really wasn't joking about this.

"There's a pay phone," she said, not wanting him to have a record of her calls. Then, realizing how dumb that sounded, she added, "All those stories of microwaves and cancer, you know. Yikes. That's why I don't own one. Can I walk now?"

"You don't like the Prince Charming treatment?"

His smile dazzled her, and Emmy had to wonder if she'd be able to stand up when he set her down.

"It's more like the Neanderthal treatment."

He stopped by a rack of cheap cowboy hats and sombreros, laughing. The rumble of his good humor vibrated through her, warming her.

Finally, he set her down near the pay phone, making sure she faced him. He almost seemed to be back to the swimming-hole Deston, a man without a care in the world.

"You make me laugh, Sunny. That's why I want you with me."

He *would* have to say something to squash all her common-sense doubts.

She wanted to ask what he'd do after their sun-soaked flight of fancy, but didn't dare. She'd be gone, back in the kitchens. He'd definitely be in New York, because she'd make sure he never had to marry her out of duty.

But what if...?

No. She didn't even dare think about it.

Okay, she couldn't help it. What if Deston fell in love with her during this vacation? What if she could get past his barriers and make him happy for more than just a few days?

What if he could adore her and their maybe-baby so much that he wouldn't care who she was and what she'd done to win his love?

The thought gave her hope, gave her sorrow.

With a tender touch, he guided her toward the phone. "You do your business, anti-cell phone activist, and I'll take care of mine. But know this..."

He placed a possessive arm around her waist, leaned down to whisper.

"...I'm not letting you go this time."

He kissed the sensitive rim of her ear, making Emmy shiver with remembrance.

Skin on skin. A hot summer night. Candlelight shimmering off the planes of his beautiful body.

He left, keeping his gaze on her, grinning.

If she tried to get away from him—yeah, right, like she really wanted to—would he follow her?

Deston really wasn't giving up.

Filled with both ecstasy and trepidation, Emmy turned to the phone and placed the call to her mama. With bated breath, she explained how she'd run into a Culinary Institute classmate right here in San Antonio. Explained how she was going to go to that friend's Houston apartment for a few days, just to catch up and try some new beef recipes from "that friend's" recent trip to Argentina.

As expected, Mama scolded her, but seemed excited about the possibility of new meat recipes that Mr. Rhodes might enjoy.

Weighed with guilt, Emmy ended the call, glancing over her shoulder to see Deston leaning against a pole, watching her as promised.

Unable to help herself, she smiled, all her hopes and dreams coming out in that one gesture.

His gaze intensified, and she could feel the sexual need—the promise of love, she thought—filling the yards between them.

Once he knew how much she could love him, how much joy she could bring to his life, everything would be okay. All these silly lies were only stepping stones on the path to their happiness.

He'd gone from frowns to smiles today, just because of her. She was absolutely sure of it.

Emmy was good for him. If he could see that, all the fabrications would disappear.

Utterly convinced, she gave him a fond wave and turned back to the phone to call Felicia and Carlota.

She wanted to tell them how she was going to win her Prince Charming.

Chapter Eight

They'd flown to Miami on the Rhodes's private jet, an aircraft stocked with posh furnishings, caviar, foie gras and champagne—which Sunny turned away during supper.

Deston was determined to treat her like a princess while awaiting news about the mysterious Cayman bank employee who was helping with the Stanhope payoffs. When he'd first asked Sunny to come with him, the suggestion had surprised even himself, but he'd warmed to the idea very quickly.

Sunny made him feel good. And Deston could sure use a diversion during this stressful trip.

And maybe, just maybe, this had something to do

with making things up to her. Maybe he was lavishing her with a getaway because he couldn't warn her about his father's schemes.

That was the most comfortable explanation.

The minute they arrived at the airport, Deston felt himself relax, separated from Oakvale by miles of land.

Then, with an efficiency Deston paid well for, a rented limo took them past the moon-rippled Atlantic waters, the palm-lined shores, the pastel and art-deco buildings that distinguished this city from any other. They passed boisterous nightclubs and colorful bistros, stylish boutiques that had closed for the night. Then they arrived at their exclusive hotel.

The Neptune rested on the beach, boasting rooms that had every luxury imaginable: a wide-screen plasma TV with surround sound, a full bar stocked with aged ports and Cuban cigars, king-sized beds with gauzy mosquito netting grazing the silken spreads, a baby grand piano. A Jacuzzi bathtub.

Sunny took a good look at the entire penthouse suite, paying attention to every last detail. Her appreciation opened Deston's eyes, too, reminding him how damned lucky they were.

Intending to spoil Sunny, who came from a family that was well respected yet hardly as wealthy as his was, he ducked into the bathroom. He filled the Jacuzzi bathtub with a potion that had been already been delivered to the room, along with the other parcels that rested on the foyer floor. The oil was a blend of cinnamon and roses, slightly foreign, sensuous. Deston closed his eyes as the steam wafted up to him.

Perfect for Sunny.

"You're efficient," she said from behind him.

He opened his eyes and turned around to find her dressed in a thick terry-cloth hotel robe. She looked adorable with her ruffled hair and bare feet.

"Did you peek in the packages?" he asked. "I want to make sure the sizes are right."

Earlier, Elaine had phoned a personal shopper with Deston's and Emmy's measurements and needs. Everything had been waiting for them, just as it'd been his entire life.

How many questionable deals had his father devised to get Deston all those perks? The thought of it made him a little sick.

"I checked everything," Sunny said, watching him with her head tilted. "Is everything okay? You seem a little...I don't know. Down."

He reached out, tugged on her bathrobe's sash. "With you around, nothing can go wrong."

She glowed, making him feel guiltier than ever about keeping the truth from her.

"Did you see that long red sheath?" he asked. "The Valentino? And the jewelry?"

"Yes, I did. They're amazing." She hesitated. "But I can't accept any of it."

He chuckled, knowing rubies and diamonds could win over any woman. "You were born to wear beautiful clothing. Up until now, I've only seen you in modest dresses, hippie stuff."

"Are you making me over or something?" She raised her chin playfully, with challenge. "I like vintage shops. The clothes have more character."

A beat passed between them. Then she bent to run a hand through the bath water.

Fancy clothes. A hideaway hotel. Caviar.

He tried not to think about using his riches to win her over, to cushion the blow once she inevitably found out that the Rhodeses had betrayed her family in business.

A rush of tenderness consumed him, heavy as the scented mist. He rested a hand on her head, smoothing her hair.

She stopped testing the water, paused. Deston jerked his hand away.

What had he been doing?

When she glanced up at him, he could've sworn there was an urgency in the way she parted her lips, in the way her eyebrows drew together.

It was almost as if she wanted to tell him something.

Just as much as he wanted to tell her.

Don't, he thought. Don't say anything that could ruin this trip. Especially if it has to do with getting emotional.

He interrupted her before she even spoke. "Why don't you hop in the water while I wrap up some loose ends on the phone. Take your time."

"Oh." She pressed her lips together, then spoke again. "That's gentlemanly of you."

The bath. Was she expecting him to take one with her even after her reluctance at the Mexican Market?

"No expectations, remember?" he said.

"I wasn't sure you'd live up to that." She grinned, stood. "Deston, about Maybe-Baby. I—"

"Maybe-Baby?"

"That's what I call our…well, you know."

Sunny crossed her arms low, over her belly, the roomy bathrobe making her seem too fragile to go through childbirth.

His mom was the same way, and it seemed that she'd never allow her husband to forget the pain she'd endured in order to bring Harry and Deston into the world.

That's right. Lots of love in the Rhodes household.

Touched by the nickname, Deston covered her hands with one of his. Together, they formed a roof over their maybe-baby.

Would a child be as scary as he'd always thought?

"How do you feel about it, Sunny? A kid."

"Nervous. For a lot of reasons. Kind of happy, too, I think." She slipped one hand into his, threading fingers with him.

"I think" sounded ominous. Why?

"I'd provide a good home for the two of you," he said.

"Would you be there? With us? Or…?"

"…or would I want you to be a mistress? Is that what you're asking?"

A breath chopped out of her. "Yes." Her voice

strengthened, and she gripped his hand. "I'm not going to be anyone's second-string player. Never."

Something was going on behind those brown eyes, something distant and painful.

He wanted to soothe her until the agony was gone, to hold her until they both felt better.

But common sense took over. His practical side had been shaped by Juliet Templeton, and he'd be damned if he ever fell into that kind of trap again: one in which he had believed her when she'd come home drunk from a party.

"I just had a glass of wine with my friends," she'd say, conveniently skipping the part about sleeping with a one-night stand.

Or...

"Deston, I want to be a girl you'll be proud of. I promise—no more parties. No more wild nights."

He'd believed every word, too, until he'd lost his temper, upset her, driven her to an early death.

"Sunny, I'll be honest. I can be faithful to a marriage, and I can give my son or daughter anything they need. But I'm always going to be a businessman, working late hours, even staying overnight at the office most times. I can give both of you my name, but I can't promise anything more."

She loosened her hand from his, moved toward the bath, staring into the water. "It's getting cold."

"Do you understand what I'm telling you?"

"Of course." Strikingly composed, she met his gaze.

"We weren't supposed to last for more than a night. I don't hold you to anything beyond that. I don't expect a marriage, frankly."

"I would. I won't have my child running around as a bastard."

His temples pounded. Why did this have to be tearing him apart? The solutions were easy.

She smiled at him, but the gesture only added to his confusion.

"Maybe we don't need to be worried," she said. "Let's talk about this *if* the time comes."

With utter calm, she ran more hot water into the tub, warming the bath.

How could she be so collected? Or was she hiding the same maelstrom that was raging through him?

What would his family think if he married Sunny? Would they pick at her quirky "vintage" wardrobe? Would they consider her an underling after they'd taken over the Stanhope holdings?

Years ago, with Juliet, he'd wanted her to change, to fit into his life more than she already did. He'd wanted her to contain that wild laugh of hers, wanted her to wear her hair in a sleek, tamed style instead of that bushy, glam-rock mess she preferred.

Deston had recognized the arrogance of his requests, but he'd loved every other part of Juliet and he couldn't stand the thought of not being with her. He'd been willing to compromise on his own shortcomings, too.

But, in the end, poetic justice had won the day.

A new thought slammed into him.

Was he actually being given a chance to redeem his attitude with Juliet by taking Sunny as she was?

Truthfully, now that Deston was gaining on his father's unethical practices, he cared less and less about the Wall of Shame in their cigar lounge. Cared less about succeeding as a Rhodes.

In Deston's eyes, his father was fast becoming less than a hero to him.

Once upon a time, the old man had been Deston's role model. Even though they fought with each other, respect and a gruff love had provided a foundation for their relationship.

But now, Deston didn't want to believe what he was finding out. He didn't want to go home and face the reality of the deceit, the payoffs.

All these troubles thrashed around his chest, echoing the whirl of the pouring bath water, leaving him helpless under the onslaught.

As Sunny shut off the tap and turned on the Jacuzzi jets, realization settled over Deston, allowing him to breathe again.

They were a universe away from their problems. Why not make the most of it?

"You're right," he said, moving toward the door. "We should just enjoy each other."

"Good." She laughed.

"Here, we can reinvent ourselves, forget our problems for a couple of days."

"That was the original plan."

Neither of them had to comment again on how those original plans had turned out.

"I'm going to make those calls," he said. "I'll leave the gown and jewels in your room. Then we can decide where to go tonight."

"Deston—"

He gently shut the door on her protests, knowing he'd feel worse if she didn't accept his gifts. All he wanted was to get some thinking done, then shower and get comfortable with Sunny.

He was going to relax even if it killed him.

Emmy glared at herself in the intricately designed full-length bedroom mirror.

The long satin sheath, diamond-and-ruby choker and matching earrings added to the perception that she'd become another woman on the day she'd met Deston at the swimming hole. Only now, the transformation was complete.

With the room's palatial furnishings looming behind her, Emmy seemed like one of *them.* One of the rich kids who'd scampered over the Oakvale lawns while she, Carlota and Felicia had climbed on shelves and peeked out the downstairs windows at their activities.

Pony rides and frilly dresses, croquet, lemonade and cake on porches.

No, that wasn't her. They were only her wishes, reflected back in a mirror.

Emmylou, she thought, you should've told Deston in the bathroom. With the way he was watching you like he actually felt more than a passing lust, you were on the edge of blurting it out, but...

He'd interrupted. She'd seen the anxiety capture him, and had, at that moment, wondered if he thought she was about to proclaim her love for him or something equally as impetuous.

His reaction had slapped her into reality.

She loved him, but he didn't feel the same way. And maybe he never would, judging from what he'd said about never falling in love again—even if he got married.

But what if he was wrong? What if he could achieve the impossible, just as she was doing?

In the mirror, Emmy saw her features soften. For years, Deston had lived in her heart, occupying his very own space. He'd always been the barometer by which she'd measured other men.

Even Paolo had failed to match up.

And, at some point, probably in cabin number five, she'd gone from eternal infatuation to something deeper. Something that was throwing her life into disorder.

But, hey. The only way she was going to get out of this emotional mess was to leave the room and join Deston. Once outside, she'd do her best to see that he fell for her. She'd make sure he wouldn't frown again.

Then, she could tell him about Emmylou Brown.

He'd be as angry as a tornado, but she'd take full responsibility. She'd convince him that she was every bit as "upstairs" as the rest of his family, and that love erased life's stations.

With one final pep talk, Emmy headed out her door and into the center of the suite. In spite of the deep Southern humidity, a fire was burning, mixing with the flow of cool air from the conditioning unit.

Wealth.

If she were at home, she'd be anxious about the wasted energy and how much it cost, but that was actually the point.

She wasn't in Texas anymore.

She wasn't Emmylou, either.

She was just a woman in love with her man.

Deston was standing near a waterfall sculpture, aiming a remote at the entertainment center. The opened curtains allowed the moonlight to wash over his broad shoulders and solid build. He was garbed in a suit, sans tie, almost as if he were a well-dressed rebel ready to walk the red carpet.

Silent, she was content to merely watch him. He was accessing the television to conjure music, the remote poised like a six-shooter.

He came across a station playing classical music, a piece that reminded her of castles swathed in sunrise clouds.

"There," she said. "That one."

Glancing over, he grinned, then froze. The song

swelled, tightening her throat. The moment was perfect: the way their gazes locked, the way he looked at her with more than temporary need.

Was he feeling more, too?

"You're a vision." He put down the remote, came toward her. "But you always are."

Inadvertently, she took a step backward, afraid to fail. Afraid he'd always be a Rhodes and she'd always be on the fringes of his life.

"Thank you." She nodded toward the speakers. "That song. It sounds familiar."

"'Claire de lune.' It actually reminds me of you in that pink dress. Remember the one you wore to the gazebo?"

"Yes."

How could she forget?

With practiced ease, Deston swept her into his arms, waltzing her around the carpet. She laughed at the romantic breeziness of the gesture, and he smiled down at her.

"This isn't really a song to dance to," he said. "It's more for swaying. Or maybe even for just standing here."

He chose the swaying option, holding her like one of the room's exquisite glass vases, making her feel just as transparent.

"You've got good technical form," she said.

"It's all those debutante balls and charity functions. Harry and I learned to dance right after we took our first steps."

The image of Deston guiding another woman across a ballroom floor floated across her mind. Emmy held back a ping of envy, until he whirled his fantasy partner around, revealing Emmy's own joyous face.

So happy.

"I know you spend a lot of time in your other home. Pittsburgh," he said. "Do you attend a lot of functions? Your parents aren't much for a party, I know."

Stick with the basic truth. "I haven't had as much soirée experience as you."

"How about other gatherings? How do you spend your night life?"

His question held a graveled undertone of darkness. His gaze reflected it, also.

"What night life?" She smiled.

He relaxed. "Got it."

Did he think she slept around? Granted, she hadn't exactly been playing hard to get with him, but that didn't mean she didn't love deeply or remain faithful to a man who said he loved her back.

"Do you think I'm a party animal?" she asked, half kiddingly.

"I don't believe so." He stilled their swaying, resting his hands on her waist as the song faded into a dream gone by. "You've got some shyness about you, Sunny. But I can't read you all that well, so what do I know?"

If you knew me, you'd run, she thought. Even if you like the idea of me right now.

She prepared herself. "Would it matter if I went against your notions of who I might be? What if I, say, went club-hopping every weekend? What if I wanted to hit every SoBe hot spot tonight?"

He didn't answer for a moment, and as another unfamiliar, violin-soft song played, Emmy's heart plummeted.

Deston Rhodes wanted *this* Sunny—the sweet socialite. And, even then, not for the long run.

Finally, he answered, grip tightening on her waist. "I've been with the ultra-social type, and we ended up apart instead of together."

The same anguish she'd seen earlier, in the bathroom, enveloped him.

Emmy reached up, tentatively cupped his jaw, wanting to comfort him. "She made you so sad. I can tell."

"It was back in college, when I didn't know any better. She was a debutante who dazzled me with her rambunctious personality, and I was drawn to her love of life. But when I brought her home, all hell broke loose. The family didn't approve of the way she joked while she ate. Little things like that. I wanted her to be a part of my life so damned much that I tried to make her into someone she wasn't and, for a while, I thought she was fine with that."

While Emmy's hand dropped from his face, she tried not to believe that this red dress, these jewels she was wearing held the same make-over potential.

"Juliet Templeton." Deston let go of Emmy, turned toward the fire. "Poor girl didn't know who the hell she was, either, at that point in her life. Who does in college? She told me she'd stop going to her parties, she'd stop dating other boys. Told me she wanted to fit in with my family. I had it bad for that girl."

Emmy moved to Deston's side, then sank down to a batch of oversized pillows.

He noticed that she'd disengaged from the conversation and hunkered down next to her. "This is the epitome of fun, right? Hearing about the exes? I'll pipe down now."

"No." She held out a hand, guided him to sit next to her. "I was wondering why you think you can't fall in love again."

"If we need to be in each other's lives for more time than we'd planned, I guess you should know why I work like I do. It wouldn't be about you."

Emmy felt so out of place in her dress.

Resting his arms on his thighs, he blocked her out. "Juliet played me. When we were together, she molded herself into the perfect society girlfriend. My family finally accepted her, and we were all happy. What I didn't know is that she was still going to frat parties and sleeping with guys. Blackout sex, I think they call it."

"I'm sorry." For more than Juliet, too.

He lifted his hands as if it didn't matter, even though Emmy knew it did.

"I found out from my friends eventually. I broke a lamp or two, then, in my bitterness, called it off with her. She did love me, I think, in her own way. That night, she went out, upset, and drank herself silly. I got to the fraternity in time to see them carting her off to the hospital."

"Alcohol poisoning?" Emmy's heart clenched for the girl.

"Yeah." Deston resumed his protective slump. "She died, and I'll carry that with me until I can't think anymore."

"Why? You didn't kill her. It was her choice."

"But I sure led her up to it, didn't I?" He finally locked gazes with her again. "So there you have it. That's me. Control monster. I've turned my eye toward Rhodes Industries instead of ruining someone else's life. Now what do you think about having my baby?"

"My mind hasn't changed at all." She was still brain-scrambled, still so unsure of everything. And now, knowing he'd previously been betrayed by a woman who'd lied to him about her true self, she was afraid.

"Hell." He shook his head. "Substantial relationships aren't my forte. Don't take it personally."

How was she going to tell him about Emmylou Brown now?

Had she been misleading herself more than she'd been misleading him? What had ever caused her to think he'd fall in love with her?

Especially after this revelation?

The fire crackled behind them, filling their silence. Another song strained through the air, this one of melancholy, yearning.

He lay back against the pillows, spreading his elbows and resting his head on his arms.

So much for painting the town as red as her dress, Emmy thought.

But she wouldn't mind a quiet night with Deston. Not at all.

She leaned her head against his chest, placing a hand over his heart, wishing she could hold on to it forever.

"I like this song, too," she said.

"'Scheherazade.'" He shifted, changing Emmy's view of her surroundings.

Deston cupped her head, stroked her hair with lackadaisical absence. "Teller of a thousand stories."

Emmy tightened her arms around him, burying her face in his neck.

The storyteller.

With a sinking feeling, Emmy knew that escaping Oakvale didn't mean she could outrun the lies.

Chapter Nine

They'd slept in each other's arms that night, eventually warmed to slumber by the fire.

Oddly enough, their time together hadn't been about sex, though Deston's body had been straining for it as they'd relaxed against each other, listening to the music, lulled by the moonlight and flames. For him, that night had been about explanations, setting most things straight.

The reason he'd revealed his heartbreak with Juliet was simple: he didn't want to hurt Sunny. Didn't want her to expect him to be able to open his soul again, letting her in.

After telling her the entire story, she'd assuaged

him with an understanding hug that had lasted for hours in front of that fire.

And it'd felt better than Deston had ever anticipated a mere hug could. In fact, allowing the story to escape the cage of his memory freed him, allowed him to enjoy being near her. It canceled out his craving for anything more than an artless touch.

Much to his surprise, they'd skipped the SoBe social scene and repeated the quiet embrace the following two nights, as well.

Who would've thought this getaway would be more about romance than carnal fulfillment?

Maybe they were both afraid to take another chance with the pregnancy question still hanging over their heads. Or maybe it was because he was discovering something much deeper between them as the days passed.

Something that scared the tar out of him with its vulnerable intensity.

Still, as Deston waited for word from his P.I. in the Caymans, he and Sunny established a routine, almost like a normal couple. In the morning, they'd walk along the beach promenade, stopping at the same sidewalk café to snack on coffee and pastries. By afternoon, as Deston kept track of his update calls from Hatcher, he tried to forget business and enjoy the parasailing and snorkeling he'd convinced Sunny to try. Then, when the sun set over the turquoise waters, lending the landscape an orange-hued burn, Sunny would choose a restaurant and give him lessons about their food. Her knowledge heightened the act of dining for Deston, opening a new world of sensation.

There was "New Floridian" cuisine, with its mélange of seafood slathered in key-lime-mustard dressing. Or Cuban food, like the *lomo de puerco*— roast pork—served with rice, beans and *tostones con mojo*—fried plantains with garlic-tinged dipping sauce.

During their meals, a bright-eyed Sunny would wax on about the art of cooking itself, transferring her enthusiasm to him. In turn, he'd be captivated by her energy, her obvious enjoyment of the hobby. As the humid hours flew by, they would flirt, joke, forget everything that was waiting for them back in Texas.

At the end of their days, a hazy comfort would settle over them, leading into the questions of the night.

Should he make a move? Would she?

You'd think they'd never been with each other before, the way they were dancing around the tension.

Deston hadn't held a woman without the benefits of sex in years. Usually, he'd be out the door after a safe, lighthearted afterglow, and that would be that.

But with Sunny, that didn't seem right.

Strangely, he was content to be with her, to steal kisses and wonder why he wasn't trying to seduce her again.

On this particular day, they were engaging in their morning pattern, walking along the shoreline on the way back from the café.

Laughing, Sunny slid her free hand into his as a wave chased up the sand toward her bare feet.

"You act like you've never been in water before," he said, guiding her to the other side of him, almost as if he could defend her against the marine attack.

"That's a lot of water coming at me," she said, nodding toward the Atlantic.

As she put a little extra sway in her teasing walk, the sandals she carried flapped against the white dress he'd bought her. Deston liked Sunny in all the beautiful clothing she'd finally accepted during the last couple of days, but he had to admit that he sort of missed her vintage style.

He wished he'd realized the same thing about Juliet's flyaway hair, her belly-baring tops.

Was it possible that Sunny was actually making him a better man?

Sure. And the Dallas Cowboys were moving to San Francisco.

They walked in companionable silence for a moment, serenaded by the moan of waves and calling birds, the sun burning off the morning mist.

Their time was running out. He could feel it. Hatcher was *this* close to tracking down the man his father was using for the Stanhope payoffs. Due to the Caymans' confidentiality laws, the detective had been running into some difficulty. But Hatcher would come through. And when he did, Deston would send Sunny back to Texas on the jet, then take a charter flight to join Hatcher in the Caymans. Steeped in business once again, he'd go back to the man he'd always been.

"What do you think about doing some roller-blading today?" he asked.

"I think you'd look cute wheeling around in those things."

"I was hoping to watch you. The entertainment value appeals to me."

"Oh, I see. You want me to fly solo." Sunny bit back a smile. "How romantic."

Was that some kind of hint? Had he disappointed her by being more of a gentleman than he'd thought possible?

"Do you…?" He shrugged. "Do you want to stay in the room?"

"I didn't mean it like that." She ran a thumb along his hand. "These last few days have been some of the best of my life. You said no expectations, and you kept your word."

"Ooof. My poor ego. You haven't lost interest in me, have you?"

"Not an ounce." She'd said it softly. "I thought maybe you didn't want me anymore. You know how some men keep their distance when a woman's pregnant? Not that I am, but… You know what I mean."

"I'm more enchanted than ever."

Whoa. That hadn't been on his agenda. But every day shone a new angle of light through Sunny, revealing colors he hadn't expected. From what he knew of Lila Stanhope, which was, by design, not very much, she wasn't the type to attract him. A quiet do-gooder who still lived with her parents.

Not exactly Juliet.

Thank God.

"I suppose *enchanted* is a pretty strong word. But," he added quickly, "if fate decides that we won't see each other after this trip, you should consider yourself lucky."

"Why's that?"

They were approaching the hotel, so they veered past a sunglass-wearing celebrity walking her two Maltese dogs, then toward the tiny path leading up to the grandeur of the modern building.

"Well, just look at the Rhodes wives." Deston helped Sunny up a small hill. "There's my mom, who's about as unhappy as they come. Then there's my sis-ter-in-law, Poppy, who's just as miserable. They both know that business played a bigger hand in their mar-riages than love did."

Emmy knew both stories well since she'd seen Leti-cia Rhodes's unsmiling face firsthand and had heard all about Harry's marriage from Carlota's and Felicia's letters. But she wasn't sure Lila would know. Besides, she was curious to see how Deston told the tale—with derision or sympathy.

"I remember Harry. Wasn't there some scandal…?"

"I'll tell you about that when we're not around other ears." He presented their room keys at the guarded gate, then led her into the hotel itself, through the atrium cum lobby with its pools and water walls.

They traveled up the manned elevator, to their penthouse suite. When they were behind closed doors, Deston continued his story.

"Harry was promised to Poppy, who was a society belle. Very proper. Very much in line with the Rhodes image. But he'd secretly fallen in love with one of the Oakvale maids."

Emmy's stomach knotted. "How dare he."

"The exact words of my mother." Deston took a seat on the massive couch. "She's got unshakable Rhodes pride and would go to great lengths to protect our image. Sometimes I think there *is* love between her and my father. A sort of mutual respect. Just like business partners."

Just as Sunny's marriage to Deston would be.

"How did he end up married to this Poppy?" Emmy asked.

Deston leaned his forearms on his knees, fisting his hands together, then unclenching. "Harry ran off with his lover. Needless to say, my dad had them tracked down and, when Harry got back, Edward the Third used his immense powers of persuasion to annul their marriage. Within the week, the maid was gone and Harry was engaged to Poppy."

Perching on the velvet ottoman across from Deston, Emmy searched his stoic features. "Why didn't he stand up for the woman he was in love with?"

For a moment, Deston's green eyes blazed with righteous heat, stirring some hope within Emmy. But then they cooled.

"Traditionally, the Rhodes family has married well. Sometimes I think we're more British than anything, what with that culture's royal-blood obsessions." Deston straightened, as if he wanted to take pride in his pedigree, too. "We're raised to be American monarchs, to carry on the good family name and preserve the dignity of the first Edward Rhodes. If word of Harry's housekeeper had gotten around…"

A tight laugh capped the thought.

Emmy took a great breath, expelled it. "Do you feel that way?"

"If we got married, your family tree would pass muster. You wouldn't have been invited to the ranch otherwise."

"That's not what I'm asking."

His jaw muscles jumped. Then he said, "If my father couldn't keep control of Harry, how could he manage our corporation? That's what our clients would ask. Appearances are important."

It was as if she'd stepped out of herself, leaving her body an empty, numb shell.

"In spite of everything, we're not a weak family, Sunny. We're faithful to each other and if that means we seem arrogant to some, that's the price we pay."

Words rushed out of her, unstoppable. "So if you

found yourself in the same situation as Harry, you'd give up your true love also?"

"Don't look at me like that. I wouldn't put myself in Harry's position. He was always the sensitive one who wrote poetry to girls. I…"

She thought of how Deston had visited the servants before he'd left, getting to know their names. "I don't believe you."

He slumped, staring at his hands, defeated in some indefinable way. "I've worked myself ragged to gain the trust of my old man. And even though half of me admires Harry's *cojones* for trying to be happy with someone who truly loved him, the other half knows without a doubt that he's a jackass."

This was déjà vu, a replay of Paolo. *He* wouldn't accept a woman "below" him, either. How could she have been naive enough to misread her Italian boyfriend's intentions? How could she have taken him for a good man when he'd only been a family puppet?

She wanted to cry, wanted to knock herself over the head for even thinking her dreams would overrule reality. But Deston had just told her in no uncertain terms that he'd never follow in Harry's footsteps.

He was watching her, probably wondering if he was coming off as "superior" to Sunny. But there was so much more to his motivations than mere snobbery. There was Juliet; there was tradition and business.

There was the unbridgeable chasm that separated them.

"Hey," he said, reaching out to place a hand on her

knee. "Harry and Poppy get along well. They both accept what has to be."

She was speechless, beaten. Seeking comfort, she skimmed her hand over her belly.

Don't worry. We'll make it just fine together.

Because there'd be no other option.

A shrill ringing split the air, and Deston reached for his phone. He excused himself, leaving her with her tumultuous misgivings.

Minutes later, a distracted Deston told her he had pressing business on Grand Cayman. He must've sensed her disbelief—the still-shuddering pain of having felt the last nail being hammered into her coffin—because when he walked her to the limo, he pressed a slow kiss on her lips.

Goodbye. Vacation was fun.

But in the room where she'd abandoned the clothes and jewels of another woman, she'd already bid him farewell.

Even though he hadn't known it.

Back at Oakvale the next day, Emmy sat on her mama's bed, telling her everything she'd learned about Argentine beef preparation from her Culinary Institute "friend."

But she had something much tougher to discuss.

"Mama, please sit down." Emmy patted the mattress beside her. "I've got to talk to you."

"You seemed agitated, but I marked that up to your

hot Mediterranean blood." Mrs. Brown eased herself onto the mattress, wrapping Emmy in her cozy basil-and-rosemary scent. "I feel the same most days for no good reason."

"It's because you have arthritis and you don't want to accept it."

Mama widened her lovely brown eyes. "Emmy-lou."

"It's true. You need to stop working. When I save up enough money, I'll get you your own place in town and...I don't know. You should take it easy for a change."

Obviously wounded, Mama shook her head. "This is what I am, *cara*. Without this job, I have no purpose."

"That's not true. You felt the same way after Papa died, too."

"Bless his soul. He still lives with me." Mama covered her heart with a palm. "In here. Just as I live in the kitchens."

Emmy sighed. She'd done a lot of thinking on the plane ride home. Harry's story—and Deston's opinion of it—had slammed together in her mind, leaving her with no other recourse than to leave Oakvale and find another job.

"Maybe," Emmy said hesitantly, "we can both retire from this place."

Mrs. Brown's body jerked as if someone had shaken it.

Rushing to finish her thought before Mama's quick

temper kicked in, Emmy said, "I've been planning a restaurant. Tuscan-inspired gourmet, straight from the streets of Tocchi, your childhood home. Think of it! On the Paseo del Rio in San Antonio someday."

"Oh, Emmylou, haven't I raised you right?" Mama slapped a blue-veined hand to her forehead. "This is what comes of your papa insisting we raise you non-Catholic. Rebellious."

"Can you honestly say you're happy here, being a *servant?*"

Mama grew serious. "You say the word as if it's the scourge of humanity. Your father would be so hurt."

"He enjoyed his work, and I don't think any less of him for that." All-consuming love welled in Emmy's chest. "I respect him for it, but I don't want to follow in his footsteps."

"I told him this, way back when we'd catch you staring out the window." Mama smiled. "Your mind was always on the horizon, never on the here and now."

Emmy fisted the bedspread. "I tried to make you all happy. I tried so hard."

As Mrs. Brown absorbed her daughter's declaration, Emmy wondered when she would have the guts to tell her about Deston, about the double life she'd been living lately.

About the fact that Emmy's period hadn't shown up yesterday—and it usually came like clockwork.

As Carlota claimed, it was time to go to the doctor.

Hey, there, Maybe-Baby, she thought. Or should I

give you another name now? A real one? No matter. I just wanted to tell you that I'm glad you're here.

Emmy swallowed a lump in her throat.

Really glad.

"I suppose," Mrs. Brown said in a whisper, "that it would do no good to remind you that the Rhodes are expecting you to stay on."

"Katrina's been assisting you for a while. She's wonderful, so don't deny it. And Fritz can take her place."

"Fritz, that good-for-nothing." Mama grinned, but it disappeared like steam from boiling water.

"Mama, don't get angry now. After I get a job on the outside I'm going to pay you back every cent for my schooling and time in Tocchi. We'll pay off our debts and save up for the restaurant. We'll call the restaurant Francesca's, after you and Grandmama."

"*Perfetto.* She would like that. I would like that."

Would she also like a grandchild? Emmy wanted to tell her so badly, since she wasn't used to keeping secrets from Mama, but the news would only send the older woman into a flutter.

Besides, Emmy should go to that doctor first.

"This is what I'd like," Emmy said, falling into the safe cocoon of her dreams. "I'd like to feel as if I'm the boss. I'd like to live in an apartment off Oakvale grounds, where I can be myself and not some person who doesn't exist for the Rhodes."

"We're like family to them, Emmylou. Don't say such nonsense."

If only Mama knew how they really felt.

"May I say one more thing before you run off to be your own boss?" Mama asked.

Here it came. The guilt trip. Mrs. Brown had perfected the art, and Emmy battened herself down for the storm.

"We never told you, your father and I, but Mrs. Rhodes loaned us money for your education. She knew you'd come back and serve them well, so she made the investment. Most people don't have employers who care so much, Emmylou. This family will take care of you for the rest of your natural life. All I ask is that you care for them, as well, by giving this more thought."

"But..." Emmy quieted her arguments. How could she leave and go against Leticia Rhodes unless she could pay her back outright? And how could she do that right now?

This definitely put a different spin on things. Until she could save some money, she'd be Oakvale's cook.

But that didn't mean she wouldn't keep wishing. Planning.

"All right, Mama. I respect what you and Papa have sacrificed for me too much to throw your kindness—and Mrs. Rhodes's money—back in your faces. And I'd never toss garbage onto Papa's grave besides."

"That's my girl." Mama enveloped Emmy in a hug,

messing her hair at the same time. "You'd never let your families down."

As Mrs. Brown stood and went about securing her chignon while humming a traditional lullaby, Emmy watched her with a heavy heart.

She'd done enough running from responsibility lately to know that it didn't feel right, didn't turn out well in the end. But what was she going to do about staying on at Oakvale for the next few years? It'd take her that long to repay her loans, even if she got a part-time job in town, as well.

Besides, she'd need all the money she could get to raise her child on her own.

Crossing her arms over her stomach, Emmy tried not to feel ill about the biggest question of all:

Was she going to tell Deston about their baby, even after he'd made it clear that he wouldn't accept Emmylou Brown as she was?

Emmy tried to take peace from the hypnotic notes of her Mama's song, just as she always had. Comfort in family.

But this time, she knew she'd have to strike out on her own.

Somehow.

At 11:00 p.m., Deston arrived in San Antonio with Hatcher, well prepared to confront his father.

But when he walked into the deserted office building, he was shocked to find the senior Mr. Rhodes sitting in Deston's leather office chair, puffing on a cigar while he leisurely went through the manila file folders on the desk.

"What are you doing?" Deston asked, thrusting his briefcase—and its important contents—onto a nearby overstuffed couch.

Hatcher, a taciturn man with flat, Teutonic features, quietly took a seat next to the case, placing a hand on it.

"I'm passing the time until my son comes home." Mr. Rhodes stroked his Santa-from-hell beard. "Why? Is that a crime?"

"Perfect opening, wouldn't you say, Hatcher?"

The blond man tapped his fingers on the briefcase.

Edward Rhodes leaned back, dropping the files. "Dammit, Deston, you couldn't leave well enough alone. Now, I give you and Harry a lot of leeway when it comes to running things, but I don't expect you to fly in the face of my orders."

"Especially when they're illegal." Deston asserted his sense of control, propping his hands on his hips. "I asked you about this before, but you wouldn't tell me. Did you think I'd let your fleecing of the Stanhopes—and other companies—go by unremarked?"

"I was hoping we could keep it in the ranks." Mr. Rhodes took the cigar out of his mouth and pointed it at Hatcher. "One of those P.I.s you hired, I suppose?"

Deston had realized that his father would catch on to the investigation at some point. He'd been attempting to beat that particular clock. But why couldn't Dad have remained out of the loop for another two days?

Ignoring his father's grumbling, Deston dove right in. "The dirty work needs to stop right now. And I'm not pussyfooting around here."

"Ah, the crusader. I thought you knew what it takes to run one of the most successful corporations in the world, son."

"You can't tell me everyone pays off future employees to sabotage their accounts and their physical properties just so someone can sneak in and buy the company at a discount."

Mr. Rhodes didn't say anything. Deston looked to Hatcher, who'd previously told him that he wouldn't like what he'd discovered.

"Deston," his father finally said, "I've got to admire your stalwart ethics. First, you refuse to butter up that Stanhope girl so she'll put a good word in with her daddy, then you launch a full-scale attack on the dark side of our moneymaker."

The reminder of Lila knifed at Deston. After he'd sent her away, he'd found the dresses, the jewelry she'd left behind. The "forgotten" items were a clear statement: It's over.

But it wasn't. He still craved her touch, her laugh, her happiness.

His baby.

Deston's gut did a whirly-swirly trick that he didn't appreciate in the least. Not at this particular moment.

"Here's how it stands." With studied calm, Deston sauntered over to Hatcher, who extracted a CD—a copy of a digital recording they'd made on the Caymans—from the briefcase. "If you put this in your computer, you'll see a banker telling a very interesting story. Something about how he's been instructed to pay certain Stanhope employees secretly."

His father didn't answer. He no doubt realized that Deston would be able to prove criminal intent if it came right down to it. At that point, the Governor in Council of the Caymans would be able to step in and authorize disclosure of information.

"I made sure the banker was well-compensated for the information, after he quit his job," Deston added. "Got to look out for the little people, don't we?"

A sprinkle of cigar ash fell to Mr. Rhodes's ample chest. The sight made his father more human, open to failure. It clutched at Deston's conscience, making him want to apologize, to ask for his forgiveness.

But he'd hold firm, dammit. If not for Lila, then for all the other people who'd been wronged.

"I never thought I'd see this day," Mr. Rhodes said. "I don't know whether to be puffing up with pride or to hang my head in shame."

"Shame's a good option."

Mr. Rhodes rumbled out a sharp laugh. "Shame because you've let me down, Deston. But every Rhodes gets a second chance. Harry used his up when he went sweet on the help. It's your turn."

Harry.

Sunny had been disappointed with the way Deston had viewed the situation. When he'd told her about Harry and the maid, she'd looked at him as if he were the scum of the earth, and he knew she was right. He'd been raised in arrogance, and he wasn't sure how to shed the shield of it.

This would be a good time to start.

He was aware of Hatcher exiting the room with the briefcase, leaving Deston to deal with the more personal issues in private.

"I'm not backing off, Dad."

Mr. Rhodes froze, resembling a man who'd realized, too late, that he'd been lethally shot in the back.

"Then," the older man said, red rage creeping up his neck to bathe his face, "I guess I can't trust any of my sons."

"And who the hell can trust you?" Deston asked, watching as his father slowly lost poise. "We've got more gold than Midas. Why do we have to sink to these levels to get more? And don't tell me that's the way it's always been, because I'm not buying it."

Mr. Rhodes bolted to his feet: tall, intimidating, infuriated. "You'd understand if you were in my place. I'll be damned if the family weakens under my guard."

"I'm not asking you to weaken. All I want is to stop these underhanded tactics." He chanced a step forward. "Do you think no one else will find out?"

Silence.

"That's right," Deston continued. "I know you've asked yourself the same thing. It's time to change. And that doesn't mean you've lost your grip on matters. It means you've got the strength to right them."

"What if I don't stop? What will you do?"

Briefly, fear flashed across his father's eyes, and Deston wanted to go to him, to tell him it'd be okay.

But it wouldn't.

"I'll take this to the authorities."

He hated himself right now. Loved himself for having the guts to go through with this.

"And," he added, "I'll see the Stanhopes and come clean with them."

Only then could he really be free of guilt.

With a long, unreadable glance, Mr. Rhodes abdicated the leather chair to Deston, taking a seat next to the desk instead. Now that he was nearer, Deston could see the sweat beading the old man's brow.

He grasped his father's shoulder, held on for dear life. "I'd die for this family, but not if this is what the Rhodes have become."

Slowly, his father nodded, and Deston breathed easier.

Still, he was restless, knowing that he needed to find Sunny again, and not because he wanted to tell her about the sabotage.

He needed to go after *her* now. Pure and simple.

Chapter Ten

The home pregnancy test was positive.

After taking it last week, Emmy had floated around her cottage, a perma-smile on her lips.

Hey, baby boy or girl. That blue stick tells me you're really there, but we both pretty much knew that, didn't we? Oh, you're going to be so beautiful. When you're made from love, that's what happens. And I've always loved your father, from the day I first saw him with his hair slicked back and dressed in that suit and tie for church. I'll love you, too, with every inch of my heart.

She came to stand before her cottage window, the shadow of the big house looming over her in the setting sun.

So what will I tell your daddy? she thought.

After making an appointment to visit a San Antonio doctor for a check-up and blood test in a few weeks, she spent the next days mulling over the situation. Carlota and Felicia were mindless with joy, fussing over her, making sure she got bed rest even if she didn't need it yet.

There was no nausea, no obvious swelling. Just an emerging yen for vinegar potato chips dipped in chocolate sauce.

She hadn't told Mama about the baby yet, either. That could wait...a long time.

First, Emmy had to decide what to do about Deston.

Her initial instinct was to tell everyone that this was someone else's child. A stranger from San Antonio, a man nobody on the ranch would know. But she'd already piled so many falsehoods on each other that her conscience was ready to fall like a house of cards.

Was it fair to keep his child a secret from him? After all, he felt strongly about giving the baby his name—so strongly that he was willing to set aside his bachelor days and marry her.

But Emmy knew how that would turn out. He'd told her about Juliet Templeton and how she'd smashed his heart.

About how his family felt about the servants.

What had she gotten herself into? There was no easy way out.

Telling him about the pregnancy would clearly lead

to him knowing about Emmylou Brown, and that would lead to absolute heartbreak.

But not telling him just wasn't right.

That's how she found herself in the San Antonio parking structure of his office building.

As Emmy sat behind the wheel of her family's rusted yet functional Aspen, she white-knuckled the steering wheel, rehearsing what she might say to Deston if she saw him.

If? Heck, during their Miami retreat, he'd talked about cars: How he liked to drive himself instead of using a limo, how he enjoyed commanding his fully loaded Mercedes Benz with its vanity license plate reading Rhodes. So who was she fooling?

Emmy knew he'd be here, especially since the Benz was still parked, waiting for his pleasure. The question was, would she get out of the car when he arrived?

The man's watch she'd purchased at a Goodwill store ticked, filling the car with a nerve-wracking countdown.

At 7:32, he emerged from the elevator, walked toward the car. Truthfully, Emmy had thought he'd be at least another couple of hours, but she'd known that it would take her that long to rustle up some courage anyway.

Do it now, she thought, forcing herself to step outside to intercept him.

And she did, just as he was pressing his keychain remote to unlock his car.

"Deston." She sounded as if she'd been running for miles.

He was dressed in a dark business suit, his tie undone, brown hair a bit tousled. A combination of tycoon and the boy she'd fallen for so many years ago.

When he saw her, his eyes lit up, his mouth winged into a dazzling smile. "Sunny?" He carelessly deposited his briefcase on the cement and surged forward to wrap her in his arms.

His touch stole her breath clean away, and she reveled in it. Why did this have to feel so right?

"What're you doing here?" he asked, leaning back to cup her face in his hands, to run his thumbs over her cheeks.

Her eyes welled up, and his face blurred. A trickle of moisture spilled down her skin, clearing her vision. He dabbed at her tears, knitting his eyebrows in query.

"I had to see you again."

"Damn, I'm…" He shook his head, then leaned down to nestle his lips against hers.

The kiss held a gentle urgency that twisted her happiness into guilt. Warm, soft, so trusting.

Emmy moved away, grasped his hands, holding them together, taking strength from him. "I'm so glad to see you, too. More than glad, actually."

"I thought maybe I'd never hear from you again. Unless…"

He drew away, his concerned gaze asking her if…

She closed her eyes, pained because this was the beginning of the end.

Then she nodded.

When he liberated his hands from hers, Emmy told herself not to look, not to dive into the heartbreak so soon. But she did, caring too much about what he thought.

He'd buried his face in his palms.

"I'm not sorry," she said, voice choked. "About having your baby, that is. I'm just sorry if it's not what you wanted."

With a chuckle, he uncovered his face, revealing flushed skin, a genuine smile. "We're having a baby?"

Confused, she answered, "Home pregnancy kits are pretty accurate, so I'm almost sure. Yeah."

Deston belted out a triumphant laugh and, as a car drove past them, he yelled to it, "I'm a daddy!"

Overcome, Emmy started giggling and crying at the same time, unable to hold back her nervousness, her relief. When Deston realized that she was happy, also, he started to scoop her up, but then tenderly touched her belly instead.

"Are you okay? Have you had back pains? Swollen feet?"

"Not yet. I won't be showing for a while."

Another car parked a few spaces away, its windows rolled down. A Frank Sinatra song, "Under My Skin," played as the driver shut off the engine and stayed seated.

Emmy remembered their music in Miami, a time when she and Deston had connected on an emotional level instead of a merely physical one. Back then, she hadn't been entirely sure he wanted a baby.

She swallowed, touched by his happiness and apparent pride.

Deston swept her into an embrace, wiping away her tears at the same time. "I suppose I should read up on pregnancies. What happens month by month, what I should be doing to make you comfortable... Damn." He laughed again. "My father's going to be beside himself."

Oh, yes, he will, Emmy thought.

With celebratory flair, Deston slowly twirled Emmy, then danced with her as Frank Sinatra crooned, turning the parking garage into a sparkling dance hall.

She was living her dream again, swaying in Deston's arms.

"Your family's going to be fine with this?" she asked, clutching his arms.

"Well, you know Dad's had his eye on Stanhope Steel, right? This is a fine way to get our families to merge." His voice was light, but he tightened his hold on her, revealing more than he'd probably intended.

"But enough of family talk." Suddenly, he dipped her a little, changing the focus of the moment. "This is our time, Sunny Sue."

Sunny Sue. Emmylou.

The silly nickname sounded too close to her real

one. The reminder pulled at her nerves all over again. She'd taken care of one problem—telling him about the pregnancy—but she feared she'd just walked into a nest of worse ones.

"Loosen up, there," he said, spinning her around until she couldn't help but smile. "I didn't realize how much I really wanted this baby until now. It's like my heart popped right open and spilled out a bunch of tiny fuzzy ducklings or something."

She merely nodded, not wanting this moment to crack apart like the fragile shell of that egg.

He must've gotten the hint to stay quiet, or maybe he was just enjoying himself too much, because they slowed the pace, danced to the stranger's music, oblivious to the surroundings.

But this couldn't last forever. A business-suited female got into the car. The couple drove away, leaving the parking structure to an occasional squeak of a tire as they rounded a corner, to the rhythm of footsteps as employees went home to lives that had to be less complicated than Emmy had made her own.

"Even without the music," Deston said, his cheek brushing against hers, "this is something of a fantasy. You're the main ingredient, Sunny."

She sighed against him, holding on to what she could.

His voice traveled over her, through her, as he continued. "Seems as if I can appreciate you anytime or anywhere, under any circumstance. Even in a parking structure."

Appreciate her. Not love her. Never love.

She stopped their impromptu dance, drawing them back to the concrete, the humidity, the reality.

"Sometimes," she said, "I think we're living more in a fantasy than a real relationship."

"Having a child makes this pretty real."

"It changes everything." But it didn't alter the fact that she still needed to tell him all about herself—if she had the guts.

But she'd already been made weak with joy tonight. Deston wanted their baby. Why couldn't she be a person he'd want, as well?

He was trying to read her with his gaze. "I can't figure you out. You're still a mystery to me, with the way you disappear and the way you won't entirely let me in."

"I wish it could be different."

Because I want to hear that you love me before I give you the truth, she thought.

"Why don't you tell me more about yourself?" he asked softly.

"Maybe if you knew the real me, you wouldn't like what you'd find."

He didn't speak for a moment, and she knew he was thinking of Juliet, the woman who wasn't what she seemed to be, either.

Something seemed to click together in his mind. His eyes revealed a shift in color, a change in outlook.

"Come to the ranch with me tonight," he said, holding her hand. "My brother's in town for some family business. I want you to be there when I announce the good news to them."

She'd known about Harry's visit, but hadn't been sure that Deston would be at Oakvale, too. "I can't."

"I've got your locket."

The place where her necklace belonged felt heavier without the souvenir of paternal affection. She wanted it back so badly.

"Deston, I've made it clear that I don't need to be a part of your family." She swallowed. "I can't come home with you."

"I thought…" He let go of her hand. "I thought we'd get married. Didn't we talk about this?"

"I never agreed." She worried the sleeve of his jacket. "I'm not about to ruin your life by taking part in your idea of marriage."

"I said I'd stay faithful."

"But you left out the love part."

Even now, the reminder dug into her, burning. She had no idea what to do. Telling him about Emmylou would make the situation worse, not better.

Finally, he drew up to his full height, green eyes stunning her with their conviction. "You're not running away from me again. Not this time. Not with my child."

"I really don't want to run." She choked up. "Believe me."

"I know I said I'd respect your need for discretion,

but having a little boy or girl overrides that. If I have to, I'll hire my private detective to get you back."

"Just like your father and Harry."

He dodged the slap of her words. She hadn't meant to be cruel, but she was desperate to remain anonymously Sunny.

"I'm not letting you go," he said on a note of finality.

"Unfortunately, this isn't a jaunt to Florida, where I can allow myself to be swept onto a jet and returned home when the fun ends." She sighed. "There's so much more to this situation than you know."

"Funny." He walked toward his car. "Sometimes it seems like there's so much less."

She had no words to answer him, but did she ever?

He waited, clearly expecting something. Anything. Why couldn't she come out with it?

"Then that does it," he said quietly, posture losing a measure of its former bravado as he shook his head and slumped into his car. "Expect to see me again, Sunny. Soon."

Without another glance, Deston shut the door then left Emmy with her hand poised on her stomach, guilt overtaking her, burying her beneath should-have-dones and second guesses.

He was at the ranch tonight, so near, so far. And he had her locket.

As his taillights disappeared around a corner, Emmy knew where she'd be tonight.

And it wasn't just because of her missing necklace.

* * *

A warm wind blew through Deston's Oakvale bedroom window while he tossed and turned beneath the covers.

Forget it, he thought, giving up the battle with his sheets. Sleep would be a miracle if it happened.

His mind and body were whirlpooling with a combination of utter ecstasy and utter anxiety.

Ecstasy, because of Sunny's pregnancy. Anxiety, because of the same thing, plus a dash of family issues.

Harry, Poppy and their two-year-old son had arrived from Los Angeles this afternoon, taking up residence in the house. Deston had missed the reunion supper, though he'd tried to get away from work earlier than usual. But the after-feast drama in the cigar lounge had been ready to roll when he'd gotten to Oakvale.

His father had lectured Harry and Deston about loyalty and all the other things that went along with being a Rhodes. He'd announced Deston's ultimatum to Harry, who'd been just as shocked and appalled to hear about his father's business practices as Deston had been.

He'd had a hunch that his older brother wasn't involved in the scheme, and that made Deston feel better. Especially when his dad promised that he'd be doing business on the up and up from now on since Deston was seeing fit to blackmail him.

The biting accusation would've hurt if Deston hadn't detected an undercurrent of respect in the old man's tone. He didn't enjoy holding the Stanhope information over his dad's head, but it needed to be done.

Needless to say, Deston would be staying in San Antonio for now, keeping an eye on matters.

So issue number one had been put on the back burner. But how about Sunny?

When she'd come to him today with her news, Deston had been bowled over.

At what point in his life had he started wanting a child so much? Had the need crept into his soul without him knowing about it?

Or had Sunny changed Deston?

He tangled a hand in the sheets, almost as if he was trying to hold on to himself, a ghost escaping and making room for the new man.

Doubts were still racing around his bloodstream. Would he be as brusque with his own children as his father was with him and Harry? Could he ever fall in love with Sunny?

But maybe he *could* love, dammit.

A bead of sweat sprinted down Deston's brow. Love? Who was he kidding?

He'd offered Sunny his hand, not his heart, and if that wasn't good enough, Deston could do no better.

He couldn't open himself up again.

Willing sleep to overtake him, Deston listened to a tree branch knocking against the house, watched gnarled oak shadows shimmy on the walls.

While his eyelids grew heavy, the tree knocking grew louder, and an odd shape took form in those shadows, as if his dreams were twining into the image of a woman's body.

But this was no dream.

Deston got to his elbows, whipping his gaze toward the window.

The silhouette of a petite female in jeans and a T-shirt emerged from the open window, making his pulse pound.

"Hey," she said, her short hair fringed by moonlight.

"Sunny? What the hell…?"

She stepped toward the bed, still bathed in a combination of darkness and muted light. Wringing her hands, she stopped short of his mattress.

"I couldn't leave things the way they ended up back at the garage."

"Wouldn't a phone call have been good enough?" As he sat up, the sheets gathered around his bare hips. "You shouldn't risk your neck, climbing up the side of the house like that. Are you crazy?"

"I know my way around the house. Don't worry."

How? He and Harry, plus a few servant kids throughout the years, had made a sport out of "window-sneaking" as they used to call it. Maybe Lila had done her share of it with Harry way back when.

"Deston." She shuffled around. "Can I just ask you a favor?"

Anything for her. "Sure."

"Scoot over?"

Heat roared over his body. "I don't have your locket in any pocket here."

"That's okay. For now, at least."

He moved over, and she kicked off her sneakers, cuddling next to him.

Deston couldn't help putting his arm around her, accepting her into every empty nook of his body.

She rested her head against his shoulder. "That's so much better."

"Sunny, we're going to have to get things straight."

"In time." She paused, and he couldn't help thinking that she was working up some kind of courage to talk. And why not? They had a lot of secrets between them.

His. Obviously hers, too.

"There's something bothering me," she said.

Had she found out about his father's payoffs?

He sighed. "I have some explaining to do."

Tilting her head toward him, Sunny didn't speak.

"It's about business," he said. "My father's been doing some awful dealing with Stanhope Steel employees."

"Shhh." Sunny placed her fingers over his mouth. "That doesn't concern me."

He pressed his lips against those fingers, yearning for more. "I wanted to tell you so badly, but... I guess the timing was never right."

"I know. I know exactly what you mean." She

cleared her throat. "I need to tell you something, also, but I'm another victim of timing."

Deston stroked her neck, her jaw, feeling her shudder against him. He'd give anything to be inside her, to be moving in compatible rhythm with her thoughts, her body.

He kissed her—a slow, hungry sip of longing.

With a stifled moan, she responded, taking from him, giving to him. She was so warm and inviting, her scent filling him with sultry contentment.

She put an easy halt to the exchange by snuggling his cheek with her nose. "Did you mean it when you said you couldn't ever love me?"

He froze, remembering how much he'd despised Juliet after her death. How much he'd hated himself.

Leaning against him, face turned toward his chest, Sunny laughed a little. "There's my definitive answer."

"I'm sorry."

"Don't be. It's like sitting down to eat chicken and expecting it to taste like steak. You can't make something what it isn't."

Her words were flippant, but he caught the sadness in them.

"I know that you deserve love," he said. "But I deserve our baby."

"And our baby deserves a good upbringing." She smiled against his bare skin. "What are we going to do?"

"Compromise?" The word reminded him too much

of Juliet, so he tried to erase it, determined never to force Sunny to go against what she believed. "Forget it."

"That might be the only way."

She tapped her fingertips on his stomach, exciting him with her innocent touch. Thunk-thunk-a-thunk. Morse code to his erogenous zones.

"So," she said tentatively. A long pause marked the seconds. "If there was a marriage, would servants be bringing us our nightly chicken?"

Was she still hung up on the Harry story? Maybe his millionaire attitude bothered her more than she'd admit.

"If you're cleverly asking if I'd fall in love with a maid and run off into the wild blue yonder like Harry did, then don't worry about it."

"That's not what I'm asking at all."

"I get along pretty well without the help when I'm in San Antonio. But if you want to live in a big house like this one, you'll need servants."

Another hesitation. "Do you consider them family?"

He drew his brows together at the strange question. "Of course. The Rhodes family takes care of their own."

"Sounds like they're property. Or children."

"Where is this going?"

"Are they? Like a brand-new car that takes you places? Or are they like a carpet that absorbs your dirt but you never notice it's there?"

"They're people." Even though he was still holding her, it was almost as if they were divided by a wall of words, ideas. "I get it. You're one of those northern Yankee liberals, right?"

"No." She hugged him closer to her. "I'm just me."

Whoever that was, she thought.

He'd given a proper answer about the servants, but she still didn't think he believed the help was on the same level as the wealthy bosses. Not after so many years of upstairs/downstairs separation.

This cemented her doubts about revealing herself to him. Even if her deception proved catastrophic, Emmy could live with that. It couldn't be worse than Deston's disappointment in her true identity.

He wasn't prepared for marriage, much less a relationship with a servant. First, his family would never allow it. Second, he would never forgive her.

Emmy could rent a post-office box in San Antonio. What if Deston stayed in contact with her that way? Or with a cell phone she could scrape up enough money to purchase? They could arrange visitation without ever meeting again…

Jeez. Coming here had mixed her up even more.

Torn, she snuggled against him as he tentatively spanned her lower stomach with a hand. Their breathing evened out, matching rhythms, slowing.

This was all she wanted. Peace. His quiet affection.

His love of the baby they'd made.

The next thing Emmy knew, hints of dawn were

teasing her awake. Taking care not to disturb Deston, she stirred.

"Sunny," he whispered, pulling her against him.

Right from the get-go, she'd known he was naked beneath those sheets—hard-muscled, tempting.

Now, with daylight sneaking up on them, revealing that dark, passionate look in his eyes, she didn't feel so safe anymore.

Staying strong, she rose out of his bed.

"Don't go." His voice was strangled.

She forced herself to concentrate on donning her shoes. "I'll be in contact. Okay?"

Muted sunlight burnished the sheets, contrasting against the tan of his skin. All she wanted to do was crawl back into bed with Deston, to stay with him forever.

"I have that locket downstairs," he said. "Sometimes I take it out and keep it with me, just to remind myself that you're real."

Her locket. *Papa.*

She actually considered staying to retrieve her treasure. Hadn't that been one big reason she'd dared to show up in the big house?

Yeah. Sure.

All she was certain of was that if she lingered one more minute, she'd be a goner.

He interrupted her emotional tug-of-war.

"If you want, Harry and I are going to Wycliffe Park in a few hours, just to take his son out for some fun. If you feel like surprising me again, that's where I'll be from eight o'clock to about ten. No pressure from the family, okay? Just…" He shrugged. "Us."

Would anyone recognize her in Wycliffe? Could she take this risk?

"Would you bring my locket?" she asked.

"If it'll get you there."

"Okay." She hesitated. "Maybe you'll see me."

"Here's to hoping."

She forced herself to leave, carefully negotiating the flat roof, the sturdy trellis that led to the ground.

All she wanted was to get back her heart.

And she wasn't just talking about the gold-plated one.

Chapter Eleven

Though Deston had said he'd bring the locket to Wycliffe Park, he hadn't really expected Sunny to show up, since she'd made a habit of avoiding him as much as possible.

Except last night, when she'd crept into his room.

He still couldn't believe it. Couldn't believe he'd acted like a gentleman yet again, containing himself, schooling his body to accept her tender touches and cuddles.

He'd been missing out on so much for so many years: Afterglow moments without the "glow" itself. Whispered exchanges in the dark. Heartwarming silences.

Now, Deston wasn't sure he was prepared to live without them.

As he sat on a bench in the park, the necklace weighing heavily in his pocket, he surveyed his surroundings: a slide that resembled a large wheelbarrow, swings that hung from the arch of a cement rattlesnake body and a merry-go-round shaped like a sombrero. Vendors hawked their wares with festive ease, and the historic fountain with its statue of Davy Crockett completed the early-morning picture.

His two-year-old nephew toddled over, clamping grubby fingers onto Deston's jeans-clad knees. "Wip cweam!"

William already had half of a Cool Whip container on his face from sipping hot chocolate. "You want another cup, Mustache Man?"

"Dare to dream." Harry, a slimmer, shorter copy of his younger brother, whirled his squealing son into the air, landing him beside Deston. "You'll go into a sugar coma, Willy."

The child hopped off the bench and made a beeline toward a coffee-and-pastry cart while squealing, "Wip cweam."

Grinning, Harry kept an eye on the chubby boy. "Just you wait, Dest. This is what married life's all about."

Married. He hadn't told his family about Sunny or their baby yet. The fact that Harry believed Deston had the ability to settle down made him think it wasn't as much of a fantasy as he'd supposed.

Hell, maybe wedlock was a breeze. After all, Harry seemed content enough as a married man, body lanky and relaxed, cheeks golden with a California tennis tan.

"You're not exactly suffering from the holy state of matrimony," Deston said.

"Never. I won't admit it to Dad's face, but Poppy's been good for me."

The sentence ended on a note of opportunity lost.

Deston hesitated, then came right out with it. "Do you ever wonder what life would've been like if you'd married Graciella? If you'd taken that chance while it was there?"

Harry shot Deston a considering glance, then returned his focus to William, who'd hopped into a lasso-shaped sandbox with two other kids. "I think about Graciella some. But you know me. I can adapt to any situation just fine. Even those crazies out in Los Angeles don't rub me wrong anymore. And Poppy and I…" He shrugged good-naturedly. "We're fine together."

Deston leaned his forearms on his thighs, watching as William clumsily scooped sand with his cupped hands and allowed it to run through his fingers.

If he let Sunny slip through his grasp, would he be another Harry? A man who'd seen his best opportunity for happiness pass him by?

A cell phone rang, and both brothers checked their devices. It was Harry's.

He got up from the bench and moved away, "uh-huh"ing into the phone. Minutes later, he returned.

"Dest," he said, "I've got to access some files back at the ranch. Do you mind…?"

Cocking his head toward William, Harry silently asked if Deston would watch his boy.

Deston nodded. "Just send a car in an hour." He rose from the bench and wandered over to his nephew while Harry left the playground, phone to his ear.

Kneeling by the sandbox, Deston found William constructing a mysterious pile that resembled a bunch of nothing.

"Sand castle?" Deston asked.

William grabbed his uncle's hand and used it to pat down the mess. "Daddy opp-ice."

For a second, Deston puzzled over "opp-ice" but decided it must've meant "office." As in Wilshire Boulevard skyscraper.

William eagerly guided his uncle's hand over the sand, casting a pair of wide, innocent green eyes at him. "Daddy home."

Deston's heart rammed into his ribs.

The little boy went on playing as if he hadn't said those earth-shattering words. An office was Deston's home, also. Would his own child grow up thinking he or she was less important than work?

Would Sunny think the same thing?

Without another sound, the two of them constructed

an entire city of lumps, naming the "buildings," pretending their cupped hands were earthmovers. Eventually, the other sandbox players left, but Deston and William worked on.

"Not a bad piece of planning," Deston said, surveying their piles.

William stood, sand sluicing off his shorts as he came to Deston and rested against his uncle's arm.

The weight of the child's body tugged at something within Deston, made him feel the responsibility of supporting another human being, of loving him completely.

He hugged William to him. In response, his nephew wordlessly cupped Deston's face with one hand.

Maybe being a family man wouldn't be so tough.

After a few moments of enjoying the simplicity of just holding his nephew, Deston felt someone watching him. He glanced up from the sandbox.

Sunny stood across the playground, leaning against the string-bean-twined monkey bars, wearing khaki shorts and a white blouse, watching him with an emotion so powerful it brought Deston to both of his knees.

With a spurt of energy, William disentangled himself from Deston, falling into the sand with playful glee.

Slowly, Deston got to his feet, fisting his hands, protecting himself while wanting so badly to open up and welcome her again.

But he knew what would happen. She'd run off, and he'd be left with his palms empty.

The mere thought pushed Juliet out of the slide-show of his memories, leaving only images of Sunny: at the swimming hole, in her pink dress, across a playground, timidly making her way toward him.

"Surprised?" she asked.

He could only nod, afraid of what would come out of his mouth. She was here at his invitation. That had to mean something, right?

"Who's this?"

William grinned up at her from his prone position, face decorated with that whipped cream plus a glimmer of sand.

"My nephew, William."

"Willssssss," the boy said, rolling over in the sand, then getting to his feet to inspect Sunny thoroughly.

"Well, hello." Sunny bent, shaking the boy's hand, then quickly brushed his cheeks. "I'm tempted to call you 'sundae.'"

"Swings," William said, grabbing Sunny's hand and leading her over to the chained seats.

She looked so natural with a child, completely at ease, happy.

Impulsively, Deston came to William's other side and took his hand. By silent agreement, he and Sunny swung William just off the ground, making the child laugh wildly.

Then Deston strapped him into a mini swing that dangled from the curve of a huge cement mushroom structure. Sunny lingered next to him.

As he lightly pushed William, he wasn't sure what to say. Sunny's mere presence stole his ability to speak.

In fact, as they made the playground rounds with William, he forgot about his locket promise. They didn't even talk much at all. Mainly, they enjoyed each other's company, laughing at William's energy, trading glances loaded with meaning.

This'll be us in a couple years, he thought. Playing with our child, being entertained by his or her laughter, knowing that we've made that possible.

Or *would* it be like this?

After the swings, Sunny and William traveled up a small hill to the top of the wheelbarrow slide. Even though she was a hundred feet away, he still felt closer than ever to her.

It scared him senseless, but warmed him just the same.

"Ready?" Her voice floated down from the slide's apex.

"Ready!" yelled William.

She was holding his nephew on her lap, legs stretched out to accommodate him. As they slid down the shiny surface, the little boy "wheee"ed and Sunny laughed.

Deston met them at the bottom, swooping William into his arms. He helped Sunny to her feet, keeping her hand in his.

"Sandbox!" William said, squirming.

"All right."

Deston let him go, and the boy sprinted back to his original location.

"What a cutie pie," Sunny said.

Her bare shoulder brushed against his arm, tingling his skin.

"I can see you with our child. I can see the both of us taking care of him or her."

Sunny walked a step ahead of him, crossing her arms as if warding off an inner chill. "Remember when I told you I won't be a glorified mistress?"

It'd been during their Miami trip. "Yeah."

"I still mean it." She sighed heavily, eyes adapting a dark distance. "I've made my mistakes, and I've learned from them. Just like you."

Deston couldn't help it. He reached out to touch a wisp of Sunny's hair, feeling the softness. "Tell me."

She smiled at him, shrugged, but he knew her wounds weren't anything to gloss over. Sunny was too complex, mysterious.

While William dug a large hole in the sandbox, she spoke.

"Simply put, I was overseas when I fell for my first love. Handsome as sin. He romanced me, took me to drink Chianti in beautiful places at midnight, took me horseback riding and told me how special I was."

"You are."

She glanced at him with a fond wariness. "I fall easily for pretty words, I guess. I didn't find out until later that his family used to be rich, and they were looking to reestablish their wealth. His mother, of course, thought I was a gold digger, so she 'unwelcomed' me out of the family. I wasn't good enough for her son, and the only other time I saw him was when he asked me to continue seeing him—as his mistress. As a woman who'd never get the full respect and love I wanted."

She turned her face away from him, guarding herself, he supposed.

"Sunny."

He moved next to her, turned her face toward him. She was gritting her teeth.

"This isn't like that," he said.

"There'd be no love. You made that clear."

"Maybe I was wrong."

She sucked in a breath, and he dropped his hand from her face, taking a step backward.

What had he just said?

His thoughts clashed, banging around his brain, his heart, like lightning and thunder.

Sunny shining her love at him through the smile of her eyes. Sunny dancing with him in a parking garage as if it were a palace ballroom. Sunny holding their child in the future with as much care as she'd held William on the slide.

Deston's mind cleared. He did have feelings, dammit. But what if they came back to bite him?

Hell, maybe if he couldn't say what he might be feeling out loud, the emotions couldn't be real.

Instead, he said, "Marry me. We'd be happy together."

She waited a beat, lips parted. Did she expect something more?

He enveloped one of her hands in his, brought it to his chest to cover his madly beating heart. "Please. I'll give you everything money can buy. We can make a good home for our family."

She raised her eyebrows in a silent "And...?"

The words stuck in his chest, immovable.

A tiny laugh was her answer. "You can't tell me what I want to hear, and I'm just the same way."

"What do you need to tell me?"

With obvious yearning, she leaned her cheek against his hands. "I love you so much. I always have."

"Always have?"

"Dest!"

Harry's voice carried through the air, and Sunny jerked away, as if awakening.

He lost his grip on her, then stepped forward, needing to feel her again.

With a helpless lift of her hands, Sunny shook her head, retreating. "I don't want you to end up hating me."

"Sunny!"

"I've really got to leave."

She turned around, walking away with swift purpose. He reached for her locket, intending to lure her back, but hesitated. Something wicked inside him wondered if she'd come back again if he kept it as bait.

"Who's that?" Harry asked, coming to stand beside Deston.

"I'm not sure anymore." Deston watched her disappear behind a stand of oak trees.

Was she running on the inside, too?

Ironic. Because Deston thought he might be ready to allow something more than simple lust to catch up.

Stupid, stupid, stupid.

Hours later, as Emmy prepped in the Oakvale kitchen, she couldn't stop the word from repeating in her head like a recurring nightmare.

"Too bad Harry showed up," Felicia said, grabbing a baby carrot before it could be chopped for the glazed dish Emmy was preparing. "But even if he hadn't, you still wouldn't have told Deston. *And* you would've conveniently forgotten that locket again, just to have an excuse to come back."

"Thanks." Emmy tossed Carlota a carrot, too, just as a preemptive measure. *And* to fill her friend's mouth.

The plan didn't work.

Carlota fiddled with the vegetable instead. "I don't believe you, Em. All this time you've been waiting for a sign that he loves you, and you leave him in the dust."

Emmy plunked down her knife and rested her hands on the stainless-steel counter. "I know I blew it again. But don't you understand? By kind-of-sort-of saying that he has feelings for me, he gave me the green light to tell him the truth about Emmylou."

"And you couldn't do it," Felicia said.

"Felicia's right," Emmy said. "Even if Harry hadn't been there, I would've backed down. Sure, I hate myself for it. But you know what would've happened."

"Oh, yes." Carlota grabbed another carrot stick and illustrated the scenario. She bobbed one carrot in a talking motion. "Emmy says, 'I'm your servant, but not in the way you're hoping for.'"

She allowed the other carrot to hit the counter in a dead faint.

"Then Deston falls down, goes boom," she said, done with her dramatic interpretation.

Felicia gave a polite clap, and Carlota curtsied. Then they noticed Emmy's dismay.

"Aw," Felicia said, "we're trying to cheer you up."

"Buck her up, you mean." Carlota bit into one carrot and talked around the food. "Em, you've got to do something because this masquerade is about finished. Everyone downstairs is already gossiping. 'I hear the younger Rhodes is head over heels for some society miss.' That's what I heard Hendrich whispering to the Hausfrau Dominatrix this morning."

"Speaking of whom…" Felicia said.

Carlota glanced at her watch. "Doggonit. Gotta go, Em."

Emmy was still back at the "head over heels" part.

"Do you think, deep down, he *is* in love with me?"

Felicia kissed Emmy's cheek. "You'll never know unless you get this over with."

They were right. She'd known it, but hearing her friends say it only convinced her more.

Both Felicia and Carlota patted Emmy's tummy in farewell, a loving habit they'd taken up lately. Then they left Emmy to her scrambled thoughts, her mish-mashed emotions.

She'd run out of excuses for telling Deston the truth, and the pressure to do so was turning her stomach.

Hi, yet again, Deston. Say, could you do me a favor and come down to the kitchens? I've literally got a bun in the oven.

Oh, sure, she thought. Be flippant about this.

But facing the truth stung too much—knowing how disappointed he'd be when he found out she didn't have halfway noble bloodlines. How nauseated he'd be because she'd pulled the wool over his eyes.

She'd only refrained from the truth because she cared about what he thought, held his opinion in such high esteem that she'd given him the power to crush her dreams.

Amazing. She'd done it again, even after Paolo.

Why couldn't she take the power back by just telling him the truth?

Mrs. Brown rushed into the kitchen, clutching bundles of fresh rosemary and basil.

"*Buon giorno.* How's my favorite cook?"

"Mama, I'm…" Pregnant? No. She needed to tell Deston everything first.

Now, while no one could interrupt them. While she still had the courage.

Emmy started to untie her half apron. "I need to run an errand, Mama. A big one." She indicated the lunch-time pizzas on the counter. "I was going to slide those in the wood-burning oven, but could you take care of it?"

"What's bothering you?" Mama took hold of Emmy's shoulders, concerned.

In turn, Emmy rubbed her mama's arms. "Nothing, after I take care of this. If I'm not back in the kitchens tonight, it means I was fired."

"What?"

"Don't worry. I'll explain everything later. I swear I will." She started to take off, then turned around, blowing her a kiss. "I love you so much."

Mrs. Brown whipped out a hand to clutch at Emmy's chef shirt, then winced because of the arthritis. "I've got a bad feeling about this."

Emmy's blood gave a great jolt in her veins. "Me, too."

But at least the waiting would be over.

Emmy kissed Mama's hands, then, to the tune of Mrs. Brown's stream of Italian ruminations about the hot blood of youth, she hung her baseball cap and apron on a side-room hook.

Just do it, she thought. Tell him.

Boy, was she ever ready this time. And she'd keep reminding herself of that until the words were out of her mouth.

At this time of day, Emmy guessed that Deston could be anywhere.

A bolt of fear struck her witless.

She was going to step foot into the big house. She was *really* going to do this.

Gathering her bravery, she took the "up" elevator, telling herself that she was every bit as good as Sunny or Lila or anyone else she'd ever cooked for.

By the time she'd alighted and traveled the service hall, Emmy was fit to take off like a third-grade science-project rocket.

She paused at the walnut door that separated upstairs from downstairs.

Here goes nothing. She rubbed her tummy for luck.

Heaving the door open, she found an empty, lifeless parlor, lined with dark-green velvet-upholstered furniture and oil paintings of Texas landscapes. Emmy crept into it. The dining room would be on the left, and she knew it'd be empty until lunch was served in a half hour.

One of the maids, Kimberly, scuttled into the room with a feather duster in hand. She stopped short at the sight of Emmy in her cooking whites.

"Hi." Emmy waved.

Kimberly merely tilted her head, wondering.

"Any idea where Deston...young Mr. Rhodes is?"

The maid pointed to a door on the opposite side of the room. The cigar lounge, where the men took drinks and smoked stogies. Emmy thanked the maid and followed the faint scent of brandied tobacco.

I'm doing it, she thought, placing her fingers on the door. Pushing it open.

He was the only one in there, thank goodness. Dressed for a more casual lunch, with dark jeans and a button-down shirt, his posture a little wilted as he stared at the infamous Wall of Fame.

She entered the room, digging her nails into her palms to keep from running again.

He must've heard her…felt her…because he turned around, his gaze lighting up, then cooling.

Then questioning, as he surveyed her clothing.

"Vintage?" he asked.

She wasn't sure if he was mocking her, but she couldn't blame him. He had to be hurt, what with the way she'd left him over and over again.

"My gear is professional," she said, lifting her chin, refusing to be ashamed. "I'm glad I found you."

"I wasn't expecting to see you again. But that's what I always think."

"I'm sorry. So sorry, Deston."

"Why do you keep coming back if you just leave?"

Emmy paused, knowing she had to go through with this. "Because I'm scared of what's happening between us. I'm scared of what *will* happen."

"Oh, darlin'." Some of the anger left the stiff set of his shoulders, and he walked toward her. "It's the same with me. Losing control has always been my worst fear, but it's not as bad as you expect."

Just you wait.

In a natural move, Deston stroked her belly, and she covered his hand. The moment encapsulated them in a bubble of protection, making Emmy believe that nothing could touch them.

And when Deston brushed her lips with his, connecting the three of them in a gentle bond, she finally thought that maybe everything could work out. Her heart finally melted, giving in.

"I'm a sucker for forgiving you," he said. "I don't know if I like that."

"Deston?"

He rested his forehead against hers in answer.

Emmy steeled herself. "My name's not Sunny."

"I know, Lila."

The door to the lounge opened.

"Excuse..." said a gruff voice. "Hey. What the hell?"

"Dad." Deston kept Emmy within the circle of his arms, and it was a good thing, too, because she was about to be swallowed by that hole that'd opened up beneath her feet.

Mr. Rhodes stood in front of the door with Harry just behind him. The older man's arms curved at his sides in suspicious readiness. Harry merely leaned against the wall, probably curious as to why the girl from Wycliffe Park was in his home.

Deston urged Emmy forward. "I want you to meet the woman I'm going to spend the rest of my life with."

"You? Settling down?" Mr. Rhodes chuckled with clear doubt.

When Deston spoke, his voice rang with pride. It tore at Emmy's heart.

"We're having a baby," he said.

Emmy couldn't help smiling up at him, even though she wanted to be anywhere but in this room. When she glanced back at Mr. Rhodes, his face had gone red. But Harry was grinning from ear to ear.

Deston added, "I'm in love with her."

Emmy sucked in a breath. She'd waited her whole life to hear those words. Without thinking, she stood on her tiptoes and flung her arms around Deston's neck.

"I love you, too," she whispered.

"I know."

"Hell and fire."

Emmy and Deston disengaged, watching as Mr. Rhodes sank to a couch. Harry nonchalantly poured a snifter of brandy and brought it to his father. The man downed it in one shot.

He aimed a glance at Emmy. "Again, who are you?"

Deston laughed. "Come on, Dad."

Here it went.

While she opened her mouth to answer, a stern-faced woman dressed in a starched gray uniform stepped into the room and interrupted, excusing herself to the Rhodes men, then focusing all her attention on Emmy.

"Emmylou Brown, I heard you were in here," said Mrs. Wagner, also known as Hausfrau Dominatrix. "I believe you're needed in the kitchens."

Chapter Twelve

Emmylou Brown?

Deston wanted to tell Mrs. Wagner, the servant liaison, that she was in the wrong room. In the wrong universe.

But then common sense shrouded him. That and Sunny's crushed face, looking up at him with a plea for understanding.

She wasn't Lila Stanhope?

Mr. Rhodes jumped out of his chair. "Deston, are you trying to get my goat just like Harry did?"

"For once, this isn't about you, Dad." He regretted the words as soon as they left his mouth, but he was hurt, his shock sliding into a distant numbness.

Sunny turned to him, keeping her voice low. "I was just trying to tell you. I wanted to so many times, but—"

"You're our cook?"

The query sounded more like an accusation. Right away, Deston knew what was going through Sunny's…Emmylou's mind.

Harry and the maid. All those questions about servants being people, too.

All the wrong answers from him.

Sunny…Emmylou…whoever she was, bit her lip, then took hold of his sleeve. Deston pulled away from her, his anger rising.

"I've been away from Oakvale for a few years, attending cooking school and traveling," she said, clearly struggling for calm. "We haven't seen each other since we were kids."

I've always loved you.

Isn't that what she'd said in the park?

Deston's mind turned, a carnival ride that had gone off the rails.

"I don't know you at all," he said.

Stricken, Emmylou Brown's hand hovered in midair, as if trying to deflect his disappointment.

He took his first good look at the woman he'd thought he'd fallen in love with. Looked at hair the color of Nigel Brown's, come to think of it, the strands made sunnier by the highlights framing a heart-shaped face. Looked at the doe eyes and Mediterranean skin obviously inherited from Francesca Brown.

Looked at the white, tomato-stained uniform of a cook. A servant.

As if reading his thoughts, Emmylou tilted her head, clearly ashamed and wounded. Why? Because she'd lied to him? Or because she was one of the help, a different breed?

Mortification claimed Deston, too. Had she changed in his estimation just because she was one of their servants?

At that point, his brain shut down, going blank with the red-yellow spin of a soundless ambulance siren.

He'd been betrayed by a woman again.

Mr. Rhodes, Mrs. Wagner and Harry had all shifted around the room like chess pieces, positioning themselves. His father had veered closer to Deston, Mrs. Wagner had retreated halfway out of the door and Harry was backing Emmylou, watching his younger brother intently.

"What in tarnation is going on here?" his father asked, skin mottled.

Emmylou gazed at Mr. Rhodes without fear. "I misled your son, sir. It's not his fault."

Yes, it was. If Deston had been able to control his libido, things wouldn't have gone this far.

Dammit, why hadn't he learned from Juliet? She'd taught him good and well never to give his heart away.

Emmylou was gazing at Deston now. All the love

she'd confessed was gathered in the pleading, dark pools of her eyes.

"He thought I was Lila Stanhope," she said softly, "and I didn't correct him. I was afraid to, because I knew the minute he found out that I was Emmylou from the kitchens, he wouldn't see me the same way."

"And how was he 'seeing' you?" Mr. Rhodes asked.

"As an equal. That's all I wanted." She smiled slightly, revealing those endearingly crooked teeth. "And it felt so good that I couldn't give it up, sir. I kept wanting to be around Deston."

For years, there'd been a crust of ice around Deston's emotions. It'd melted during these last few weeks, but the barrier was still there: sharp as a razor, but fragile just the same.

"I wanted to be around her, too," Deston said. He turned to his father. "We kept everything a secret, mainly because I didn't want you nosing in on my every move. You wanted me to romance Lila Stanhope, but I wasn't about to give you the satisfaction."

Emmylou cocked her brow, obviously rattled by his own little secret.

"Is this what had you so fired up about Stanhope Steel?" Mr. Rhodes asked.

"Partly. But there's more to it. Much more."

"Right. A baby." His father cursed. "How could you allow one of them to trap you like this?"

One of them.

Deston narrowed his eyes in response to the ugly phrase.

Emmylou clenched her jaw. What kind of shame had she grown up with as "one of them"? More disturbingly, did Deston and his ilk sicken her, deep inside?

He couldn't blame her. *Was* he as snobbish as his father, without even realizing it? Was he as cluelessly patronizing?

Most importantly, had he unknowingly given Emmylou good reason to fear his reaction to her real identity?

No, he wouldn't make excuses for what she'd done. Her actions were incomprehensible, devious.

Embarrassed anger forced Deston to say, "The Rhodes family and their servants aren't exactly different species, Dad."

From his spot behind Emmylou, Harry grinned and focused on the carpet.

Mr. Rhodes dismissed Deston's comment with a chuff, and Deston suddenly saw himself mirrored in his father's arrogance.

"Typical," the old man said. "Everyone's entitled to our money, aren't they? And if they have to seduce their way into a fortune, they'll do it."

"'They'?" Deston shot a disgusted glance to his father. "Now it all makes sense, doesn't it, Harry? The way we were raised to ignore the help, to separate ourselves. We're a family of bigots."

"Don't get holier-than-thou on me." Mr. Rhodes hefted a great sigh and turned to a simmering Emmylou. "I'm going to get your mama up here and we're going to have us a talk."

The condescending paternal figure. Deston couldn't help grimacing.

His father continued, putting on the "wounded act" that Deston knew all too well. "I don't understand how Nigel Brown's daughter could turn out this way. Your daddy was a fine man, stalwart, upright. He'd be turning over in his grave if he knew about this."

All Sunny's talk about her father took on new meaning for Deston. How she wanted to please him. How much she loved him.

"Back off, Dad." Deston brushed past him, making his way toward Emmylou. "We're going to talk about this on our own. Figure out what's what."

"What's to figure?" Mr. Rhodes aimed his next words over his shoulder, blindly addressing their servant liaison, who was still standing by the door. "Mrs. Wagner, get Mrs. Brown up here pronto."

The gray-uniformed woman clipped a nod at her boss, but before she left, Deston caught the censure of her tightened lips. Not surprisingly, his dad's feelings about the servants sure hadn't pleased her.

Deston was out of patience with this entire drama. He grasped Emmylou's wrist and started to lead her away. "You play this out with Mrs. Brown. I'm talking to Emmylou alone."

"This is a family concern," Mr. Rhodes said, belting out the words. "We'll keep this contained."

From his corner, Harry spoke up. "Just like we did with Graciella."

"Shut your drain, Harrison." His father held up a threatening finger.

"Watch it, Dest," Harry said, casually crossing his arms over his chest, "if you don't keep standing up for yourself you'll be engaged to a Houston socialite within the hour."

"Come on," Deston said to Emmylou.

"Wait." Harry again. "We need to take care of technicalities first. Dad, go ahead and fire Emmylou. That's the first step."

"Dammit, Harry."

Deston's older brother rolled his eyes in mock exasperation. "I'll be a true Rhodes and take care of it then. Emmylou, consider yourself fired."

"Thanks for the near-closure," she said, tone weary.

While Mr. Rhodes picked up Harry's gauntlet of challenge by raising his voice and giving him a piece of his small mind, Deston hoped the stress wasn't exhausting Emmylou's body, their baby.

"You okay?" he asked, sounding far more gentle than he felt.

Her eyes widened, probably because she hadn't expected any kindness whatsoever. "All I want to do is explain."

"Believe me," Deston's voice reflected his anguish now, "I'm expecting it."

As Harry and Mr. Rhodes continued scrapping, Deston guided Emmylou toward the door, only to be stopped by Mrs. Brown, who was rushing in.

"Emmylou?" She was wringing her hands, furrowing her brow.

"I'm sorry, Mama." Emmylou broke away from Deston to hug Mrs. Brown. "I did a really stupid thing."

The older woman rocked her daughter in her arms. "Wagner told me everything she heard. You're having a baby?"

Emmylou pulled back, slid a bashful glance at Deston. He nodded, a spark dancing inside his chest every time he was reminded of the fact.

He wouldn't allow happiness to be taken away from him.

Mrs. Brown started crying, great sobs of joy, which drew the attention of both Harry and Mr. Rhodes.

"Mama." Emmylou comforted her. "I couldn't tell you. I knew you'd be so disappointed."

"Disappointed?" Mrs. Brown held her child's face. "I'm a grandmama." She addressed the room, completely oblivious to the battle being waged. "A grandmama!"

"Mrs. Brown…" Deston said, eager to get the answers due to him.

"And you," Mrs. Brown said, frowning at Deston. "How exactly did this happen?"

"That's what I'd like to know." Deston ran a frustrated hand through his hair.

Mr. Rhodes bore down on them. "Your daughter's found a way to get out of the kitchens and into my son's bedroom."

"Mr. Rhodes." Mrs. Brown held a hand to her chest, obviously flabbergasted.

"Dad—"

"Nigel's family has been loyal to the Rhodes clan for generations," his father said. "It's a shame his daughter turned out to be a gold digger."

Emmy froze. Voice tight, she said, "I'm a lot of things, but that's not one of them."

Chaos broke out, accusations flying, hitting their targets. But only Mrs. Brown's words had the power to still the air.

"I always did tell Nigel you were a pompous, overzealous *bastardo*."

No one moved. Especially not Mr. Rhodes. Deston took a grain of satisfaction—and pity—at his father's hit-and-run expression.

"There," Mrs. Brown said, her Italian accent intensifying in her agitation. "That was the beautiful thing about my Nigel. He was a pure man who unfortunately couldn't imagine himself taking any other path in life. He never wavered from his duties, never wanted to besmirch his honor by quitting, and I was willing to carry on the tradition for him because I truly love life here on Oakvale. But you've spoken against my Emmylou—Nigel's Emmylou—sir. So. In the name of my dear husband, you can press your own suits, cook your own meals, kiss your own *glutei*."

With innate dignity, she turned to Emmylou. "I'll be packing."

"I'll join you soon." In spite of everything, Emmylou was grinning at her mother, as if some sort of blockade had been demolished.

Mrs. Brown left the room in its stunned silence, and Deston couldn't help feeling a little sorry for the old man. He was getting it from all directions lately.

"You might want to rethink your position on the help," Deston said, shrugging. "They're getting kind of uppity."

As Mr. Rhodes grew even redder, Deston finally led Emmylou out of the room, intending to take her somewhere private—anywhere—to ask her why she'd lied to him.

To find out what the hell they were going to do now.

They ended up in the vegetable garden, bringing Deston back to a time when he'd actually met Emmylou Brown—a woman with a sore throat and a body-swallowing outfit that showed no details.

And, oddly enough, he'd even seduced Emmylou with her own food. Her masquerade had been well thought out.

Fool.

Under a graying Texas sky, they faced each other. Deston and Emmylou.

But even in his anger, he wondered where his Sunny had gone.

* * *

"I held back my questions in front of all the others," Deston said, posture livid. "And I hope that gave you some time to think up answers."

"I didn't need it. I'm going to tell you everything."

The revelation of her identity couldn't have come at a worse time. Before Mrs. Wagner had burst into the cigar lounge, she'd been so close to telling him the truth, but then the situation had spun out of her grasp, leaving her with no choice but to wait. Again.

But this is where it'd stop.

She tried not to be intimidated by him—the boy who'd grown into such a handsome, complicated man.

"Do you really think I'm so damned shallow?" he asked, voice graveled.

"Maybe I did underestimate you, and, among other things, I'm sorry for that. But I'm not sorry about falling in love with you. For having your baby."

"Dammit all." Deston shook his head.

"I already told you why the charade started. That day at the swimming hole, I couldn't believe my luck." She felt a daydreamy smile settle on her lips, tried to fight it. "Here you were, Deston Rhodes, talking to me. You *noticed* me. Then you called me Lila."

"That's when you should've corrected me."

"I actually did, at first. I said something like, 'I'm not the woman you think I am.'"

He lashed out at her. "That's right. In a lot of ways."

She actually winced, knowing she deserved every sting of deserved anger. "My intentions were never greedy."

"I'm not enraged because of money. You never asked me for anything but affection. What gets me is your lack of faith in how I'd react."

How could he think it was easy? She'd spent so much time agonizing over telling him, then weakening every time she tried.

"Can you honestly tell me that, at the swimming hole, if I'd said, 'Oops, sorry buddy, but you're checking out the family help, here,' you would've stuck around? Would you have been just as intrigued?"

He didn't say anything.

It felt as if a giant gavel had slammed down on her, a final judgment, her worst fear coming true.

"This is what I was afraid of. Me not being good enough for you." Emmy's stomach turned.

Don't fret, baby, we'll make it through.

He was still silent, caught in his own web of thoughts and doubts.

"That first night," Emmy said, feeling as hollow as the belly of a cold oven, "I came to you because we both agreed it was short-term. You were leaving, and I thought...well, that I'd take a chance."

She contained a quiver of remembrance. "You desired me. That was no secret. For years, I'd dreamed about you. Silly fantasies where I was a Cinderella.

You can understand how appealing that might've been, with me growing up in my thrift-shop clothes because my dad's debts were piling up and we didn't have the money to pay them. With me wishing I could be one of the Oakvale guest girls with their beautiful dresses and shiny shoes. It wasn't their material possessions that got to me—it was the way those girls moved, as if they knew they were special, admired. When you talked to me, held me, at the swimming hole, I thought I could be that way, too."

"I wish you'd told me about your dad's bills. I could've taken care of that."

"No, Deston. I didn't want your jewels *or* your charity."

He hesitated at her firm denial. "You ran away that night at the gazebo."

Like so many others. "Every time I left you, it was because I came to my senses. I always told myself that you'd be gone soon, that you'd forget about the girl you'd seduced back home. That you'd move on to your next woman."

When he glanced up at her from beneath a lowered brow, his gaze held so much self-disgust that Emmy wanted to absorb it from him. But she wasn't sure she had anymore room in her conscience.

"As my feelings grew from daydreams to real love, I realized that I'd dug myself so deep that there was no way to stop without damage. Especially after you told me about Juliet. About Harry and the maid. I was convinced that you wouldn't be able to see past our stations in life."

Deston's rage renewed itself. "Why the hell couldn't you just trust me?"

Emmy refused to give into the horror of this nightmare-in-motion. She'd lost his love. She'd been right about everything. But she wouldn't let this kill her. Even if she felt halfway beaten already.

Deston seemed affected by the look that must've been on her face. In a naked moment, he softened, reached out a hand to her, then jerked it back, cursing.

"Why couldn't you trust in what was growing between us?" he asked.

Emmy fought her tears. "Remember when I told you about the man I'd met overseas? The one whose family thought I was after his money?"

He frowned, recovered. "Did you make that up?"

"No."

Deston paused. "I guess he didn't help matters. Probably taught you a lesson or two about betrayal. Lessons I learned, too."

During the ensuing pause, a frail herb-laced wind floated between them, stressing the tense silence.

"Have I put you back at square one?" Emmy asked. "Do you still think you'll never fall in love again?"

This time, when he looked at her, his broken heart was reflected in the slivers of his eyes. The shards, breaking apart the green irises. The splintered pain.

He was hurting from more than just the charade, wasn't he?

"I can't be sure about love anymore," he said. "It's not what it's cracked up to be."

A sob tore through her body, overtaking her with complete grief.

"Don't cry," he said, fisting his hands in obvious helplessness.

"I'm sad for you, Deston."

"Why the hell is that?"

She could hear the cracks in his voice, the fractures widening under pressure.

Talking around her tears, she said, "I'm sad because I think you're always going to find an excuse to avoid love. I've made it easier than most women will, but you're never going to expose your heart again."

His repressed fury exploded. "You're wrong. My emotions don't control me. They're not going to lead me into forgiving you for something so cynical, so…"

He couldn't say anymore. God. She'd reached inside of him, found the core of his greatest misgivings and cradled it in her protective hand.

"Am I right?" she said, enlightenment dawning over her features. Moisture glimmered on the cheeks he wanted to caress. Tears spiked her lashes, making her look heartbreakingly vulnerable.

"Could it be that you've been looking for an excuse all along to avoid an emotional commitment?"

"Don't turn this into something about me." He'd been laid open, bared, and the feeling left him powerless. "You manipulated me, remember?"

"Oh, believe me, I'm quite aware of my faults."

He wished he could tell her that he wanted to forgive her, wanted to start all over again.

But back at that swimming hole, if she'd told him she was the Oakvale cook, how would he have reacted?

No sense asking himself, because he damned well knew. He would've tipped his hat, regretted the bad luck of having such a lovely cook and gone back to the office.

And that's exactly what he should do now. Who knew what else Emmylou Brown had up her sleeve?

He reverted to a board-meeting demeanor, comfortable in his protective world of all-business. It's the only place he could think to turn, to shield himself. "I suppose we'll need to talk about visitation."

Emmylou covered her mouth with a shaking hand, closed her eyes, nodded, accepting what she probably thought was inevitable.

Something deep inside Deston shook open, connected to her dreams, her innocent hopes. Something did forgive her. But he'd given that something fresh air for the last few weeks, and it'd steered him wrong.

It wouldn't happen again.

He started to walk away, stopped, then thought better of lingering.

"I really do love you," she said, voice trembling but staying strong with her conviction. "That wasn't a lie."

He didn't want to turn around because, if he did, he'd lose his bearings. His determination to remain untouched for the rest of his life.

The wind rustled through the plant leaves, skittering over his conscience.

He couldn't look back. Not if he wanted to stay whole.

Their baby.

The baby he wanted to love.

Pulse skittering, he glanced over his shoulder.

But, understandably this time, she was already gone.

Chapter Thirteen

Mama packed the last of her clothes in her scuffed sixties-era suitcase, then took one last glance around her spartan room.

"I wonder," she said to Emmy, Felicia and Carlota. "Is it too late to go back to the kitchens, after all?"

The young women had all been standing near the door, hugging each other goodbye.

"Mama," Emmy said, keeping an arm around each of her best friends, unwilling to let go. "You quit, remember? And it wasn't just an ordinary notice. You went out in a blaze of kiss-my-*glutei* glory."

"Yeah, Mrs. Brown," Carlota said, voice wobbling.

She usually kept her cool, but Emmy's leaving clearly upset her.

Mama tossed up her hands in surrender. "Why would I want to stay after what that man said about my Emmylou anyway?"

Felicia silently walked over to Mama and her suitcase, grasping the handle and hefting it off the bed. They'd already loaded up the clunky Aspen with their other meager belongings, and Emmy had persuaded her friends to flip a coin to see who would take over her cottage.

Felicia had won. Not that she was cheering about it.

The baggage-laden blonde traipsed out the door, but Carlota stayed, giving Emmy one last hug.

"You're not going to leave Oakvale without him," she said.

Emmy held back tears. "Is that a vision?"

Carlota gave a final pat to Emmy's stomach. "Anyone who believes in true love can hope."

With a bolstering wink, she left for the car, where they'd say their final good-byes.

Now Mama and Emmy were alone.

"I'm so embarrassed for you, Mama," Emmy said. "I didn't mean to bring you shame."

Mrs. Brown tucked Emmy's hair behind an ear, soothing her daughter. Emmy's heart rate smoothed out. She was so lucky to have people who cared for her. People she loved right back, even if Deston wouldn't be one of them.

A jagged sense of loss pierced her.

"Emmylou, you're my little angel." Mama's eyes sparkled. "Maybe your wings melt every once in a while, but that's only because you're flying too close to the sun."

"Is that your way of saying that I had no business being with Deston?"

"Oh, no." Mama's pride manifested itself in the stubborn set of her shoulders. "I'm sorry if you were raised to think you were below anyone. Your papa and I never meant that to happen. I only wish you had gone about this situation with Deston in a more…practical manner."

"Even I can't believe I lied to him all that time." Guilt pinched at Emmy, agitated her to the point of restless mortification. "It doesn't seem like something I would do."

"But you did it. No turning back," Mama said, patting her daughter's tummy and linking arms with her as they left the room.

Once again, Emmy felt the need to apologize. She'd been repeating I'm-sorries to Mama ever since joining her in the packing process.

"Mama, I'm—"

"Calm down, *cara*. There's no doubt that I don't like being left out in the cold when it comes to my daughter, but now's not the time for getting upset. We've got too much to take care of."

"Like deciding our futures."

At least they'd already determined which budget motel they'd stay at in San Antonio. Tomorrow, they'd hit the town, looking for cooking jobs in restaurants, gradually saving up to repay their debts. Then, one day, when they were all caught up, maybe, just maybe, they'd open that restaurant.

In the meantime, they'd stick together, saving for Emmy's baby and a home of their own.

As they emerged outside, her pulse beat like hummingbird wings. The skies were a gloomy gray, the wind having picked up enough to blow their hair around.

Adrenaline flowed. Remorse chilled her. Anxiously, Emmy fidgeted with the car keys, dropped them on the ground.

"Are you okay to drive?" Mama asked.

"Of course." Sure, she was shaking, her nerves twisted like frayed rope, but she couldn't wait to barrel out of here, into their new lives. She picked up the keys.

"If I could take the wheel I would, but…" Mama didn't drive. Never had. Had never seen the need.

"Don't worry about it."

Mama cast her a suspicious glance, then stroked Emmy's hand, a lullaby of touch. "Do you mind if I stop by the cottage for a moment? I want to say goodbye to Nigel one last time."

They'd spent so many years in that sweet little abode together. "Of course, Mama. I'll meet you by the car with Carlota and Felicia."

They separated, only to meet up twenty minutes later. With Emmy's best friends waving a melancholy farewell, Emmy gunned the Aspen's accelerator, desperately wanting to leave Oakvale behind.

"You're going fast, Emmylou."

"The better to be out of here," she answered.

"Where's your seatbelt?"

"Right." Emmy struggled to put it on.

The big house loomed in the rearview mirror, growing smaller and smaller, making Emmy's heart shrink with every passing second.

She still couldn't get into that seatbelt.

Near the end of the long, winding driveway, just as they were about to cross the threshold into a new life, something in the middle of the road distracted Emmy.

A white-tailed deer. It resembled the one Emmy and Deston had seen together on the first day they'd met at the swimming hole.

That first innocent day.

When she swerved to avoid it, all she heard was her mama's scream. Then she saw a tree, a burst of steam, the green grass rushing to meet her.

"Emmylou!"

Then she saw nothing.

Meanwhile, in the cigar lounge, Deston had retrieved Emmylou's locket from the drawer of an antique walnut desk, where he'd housed the jewelry after their park meeting. He was rubbing the faded gold with a thumb, fingering it as if it could conjure up the night he and Sunny had made love.

Not Sunny. Emmylou.

No matter how much he thought about it, she was the same person. She hadn't changed with the shift of name and social class.

He was the one who'd altered in attitude. Deston still wasn't sure that was a positive thing. Did this emergence of emotion in his life make him weaker?

Or stronger?

A pair of perfectly manicured, pale hands set a full teacup and saucer on the end table in front of Deston. He glanced up to see his mother, her spa-enhanced skin smooth and cool as a museum statue, her dark hair swept crisply into a fancy bun.

"Have some tea," she said. It was a maternal command, no-nonsense.

Deston tucked the locket in his button-down pocket, picking up the steaming cup just to give himself something to do. "I appreciate it, Mom."

Leticia Rhodes folded herself onto a velvet settee, right next to Mr. Rhodes. The two of them were a warped fairy tale: A scheming Santa and a Snow Queen.

"What do you say we work this out, boys?" Mrs. Rhodes said, propping her clasped hands on her lap.

The mediator. "What's to work?" Deston asked. "I'm leaving Rhodes Industries."

"Because I accused your girl of going after our money?"

His father clamped his teeth down on an unlit stogie, going through the motions since the Mrs. didn't cotton too well to actual smoking. Traditionally, women weren't even welcomed in the cigar lounge, but Deston had the feeling that his mother had stayed away all these years because she didn't like the smell more than anything else.

"Dad," Deston said, running a hand over his jaw, "you don't get it, do you? It's not about your ill-conceived comments. Not all of it. Our problems go a lot deeper."

Mr. Rhodes shifted under his wife's steady stare.

Deston continued. "I'm talking about the way we see ourselves. Our family isn't royalty. We're not so much better than everyone else. And I won't follow in Harry's footsteps, dammit."

His dad whipped the cigar out of his mouth. "You want to marry the cook?"

The question shook Deston anew. What the hell *did* he want? If he married Emmylou, it wouldn't be a farce, a mere arrangement.

It'd be because he felt something for her.

But felt what, exactly?

"What if I did want to marry her?" Deston asked. "Would that taint the family name forever?"

"My boys are going to end up killing me," Mr. Rhodes said, cigar seeming to stick out of his heart as he fisted a hand over it.

"Now, Edward, don't exaggerate," Mrs. Rhodes

said. "Seems to me we've got a choice to make. Lose our son or lose our dignity."

"Thanks for your support, Mom." Deston shook his head.

"I don't intend to lose either," she said, still unruffled. "It's all in the approach, I believe. If we were to treat Ms. Brown as an underling, that's how it'll be. But we can choose to treat her as someone our boy treasures. Someone who's finally getting him to settle down. A woman like that is rare."

Was this it? *Had* he decided he could spend his life with one woman, exposing his heart to more pain such as that he'd felt this afternoon?

As Mr. Rhodes listened to his wife, the cigar dipped downward through his fingers, losing stature. "You're in favor of this match?"

"Would you rather Deston lived life like Harry?"

For the first time in years, his mother broke out of her restrained composure, voice raised and shaking. Deston had seen her like this only one other time, when a condo developer had proposed tearing down a children's center in Wycliffe. And guess who'd won *that* battle?

Mr. Rhodes reached out to his wife, using his cigar-free hand to stroke her knee.

Deston hadn't known that his mother felt so strongly about Harry's dilemma with the maid. Why hadn't she said anything before? Had she changed her mind during these last few years? Or had there been husband-and-wife arguments behind closed doors, resulting in those separate bedrooms?

With a shock, Deston realized that he didn't even know his parents as real people.

She touched her husband's hand with the tip of her fingers, then straightened her posture. "Deston, don't quit Rhodes Industries. We'll come to some sort of compromise."

He swallowed away his emotion, feeling it settle in his stomach. "As long as 'compromise' doesn't include giving up my child—" or Emmylou? "—I'm open to talking."

"Edward?" she said, laying her entire hand over his.

"Stay with us, Deston," his father said.

Was this the first step in Edward the Third's journey to looking past a person's station in life?

Maybe Deston would stick around just to see the miracle take place.

Deston set down his untouched tea and stood. "I've got work to do, if you don't mind."

"Good," Mrs. Rhodes said, obviously thinking that he was going to chase after Emmylou. "I'll see that Francesca Brown doesn't leave, either."

Mr. Rhodes got a whimsical expression on his face. "I do like those beef dishes they whip up."

That's the closest thing they'd get to an agreement, he suspected.

As he left the cigar lounge, he didn't bother telling

his mother that maybe there wouldn't be a marriage. That he was still so damned mixed up he wasn't sure about anything.

Nonetheless, Deston headed toward Emmy's little cottage near the vegetable garden. The sky had turned a silver-bullet gray, wind thrashing at the trees. The atmosphere was discomfiting.

Each one of his steps grew more urgent than the last one. Maybe he was going to bring Emmylou back.

To...

What? Question her again? Make more excuses to stay emotionally distant, just as she'd accused him of doing?

Deston slowed his pace, consumed by his doubts.

And that's when a black Lexus sped up the driveway, skidding to a stop as it drew parallel to Deston. Harry blasted out of the driver's door and ran toward his sibling.

"Get inside with me!" he yelled.

Terror struck him because of Harry's panic. "What's wrong?"

"It's Emmylou." Harry was panting, yanking at Deston to come with him. "I called 911."

"Nine-one-one?" Pure horror shot through him, leaving Deston frozen and electrified all at once. He and Harry ran to the car, hopped in, flew down the driveway while Harry talked in breathless staccato phrases.

"Driving fast...Mrs. Brown fine...oak tree...deer run off..."

Deston put together the facts—Harry had been leaving the ranch in order to escape Mr. Rhodes after the Emmylou incident. He hadn't wanted to be around the snobbery, had wanted to shrug off the remaining resentment before seeing his wife and child again.

And he'd come upon the accident while leaving the ranch.

When the totaled Aspen came into full view, Deston sucked in a horrified breath. The steaming hood was crunched into an ageless oak tree that shaded the entrance gates.

Then he saw Mrs. Brown bending over a limp body.

Deston jumped out of the car before it had even stopped, stumbling toward her, grief knifing at him.

"Emmylou?"

His voice was garbled, but it drew Mrs. Brown's attention anyway.

The older woman was sobbing, her Italian accent thick with emotion. "She didn't have her seat belt buckled. I told her to do it, but she was in such a hurry…"

Deston bent to her side, afraid to touch her. Emmylou's skin was dirt-streaked, and there was a gash at her hairline, dripping tears of blood onto her forehead. She clutched her stomach, curled into a fetal position on her side.

Their baby?

She moaned.

"Oh, God, no. Emmylou? Emmylou, answer me."

Was she just in shock? How did that work? Or was something *really* wrong with her?

Harry rushed over to them. "I'm going to see if anyone in the big house can help." And he was off once again, squealing up the driveway.

"Where's the damned ambulance?" Deston asked no one in particular while he gingerly touched Emmylou's hair. Her beautiful, soft hair.

She stirred under his touch, lips pursed in what was no doubt pain.

An odd memory assaulted Deston: the flash of her smile, her adorably imperfect teeth. Now he knew why she hadn't been able afford braces.

God, she'd lied just to be near him. How much guilt had she suffered? Why hadn't he been able to grasp the extent of her feelings for him before now?

Dammit. Dammit all.

There was so much he wanted to tell her, so much he wanted to still experience with Emmylou.

"Can you hear me?" he asked.

"Deston?" she whispered.

Or maybe he'd imagined it, because her lips had barely moved.

Please, God, please have her be okay, he thought. I'll do anything if she and my baby are fine.

He remembered Juliet on that ambulance stretcher, remembered how he'd brought her to harm, also, because of his inability to commit.

To accept.

"Emmylou?" He bent lower, brushing his lips against her ear, careful to make sure he didn't move her. "Don't you dare leave me."

Her eyelashes fluttered, and Mrs. Brown gasped, crying even harder. She got to her feet and started pacing. In the distance, the scream of ambulance sirens cut the darkening air.

Emmylou moved her mouth, trying to say something, but he could tell the effort was wearing her out.

"Shhh. We'll have plenty of time for explanations later." Explanations like why the hell she'd been driving like a maniac. "Right now, I want you to concentrate on holding on to our baby, making him or her safe, okay?"

"Mm-hm."

Stubborn woman, he thought, his heart welling up. She'd stopped trying to talk, but was fighting to keep her eyes open, to see him.

"I'm here, all right," he said. "I'll always be here for you."

She sighed, and the wall of safety he'd built around himself, stone by stone, crumbled.

Unchecked, a tear slid down his face. "I've got something for you."

He fumbled for the locket as the sirens got louder.

When she caught sight of the tarnished gleam, Emmylou closed her eyes, as if committing the sight of him holding her heart to memory. When she opened them, she was smiling a little.

"I'm going to keep this safe," he said. "And when I can hold you again, I'm going to put it around your neck."

"Cinderella's slipper," she whispered, surprising him with the clarity of her words.

"Save that strength," he said, caressing the dirt from her face.

She took a deep breath, batted her eyelashes in preparation then struggled to sit up. "I love you so much, Deston. I didn't mean to—"

"Quiet, Emmylou." His throat burned as he coaxed her to stay still. "I love you, too. More than my own life. If you don't rest and get better, I don't know what I'll do with myself."

He meant every word. But even thinking about life without Emmylou wasn't an option. She was going to be fine. Their baby wasn't going to be harmed.

He was going to be the best husband and daddy in existence.

Emmylou nestled her hand into his grasp, fitting it inside his perfectly, her body made for his.

Just like Cinderella and that damned glass slipper.

Deston tried to speak around his unleashed emotions. "When we get married, it's going to be real. It's going to be forever."

The ambulance pulled into the entrance just as Deston's family arrived in the car. The rescue workers sped toward them, equipment in tow.

"I'll be with you," Deston said as a paramedic chased him off and started tending to Emmylou.

Time trudged by as they checked out Mrs. Brown, also. When she'd been cleared of injury, she wandered over to Deston, looking lost.

He opened his embrace to her, his future mother-in-law, comforting her, staying strong but not distant.

Not anymore.

His own family—Dad, Mom and Harry—circled around them, too, lending more courage, welcoming Emmylou's family into his own.

As the rescuers guided a still Emmylou into the back of the ambulance, Deston even thought he saw the shape of an old, dignified man leaning against the oak tree, shadowed by the crumpled hood of the Aspen.

Nigel Brown watched his daughter, endless love reflected in the proud tilt of his chin.

Deston grasped the locket, holding it over his chest as the older man fixed his gaze on him.

He winked, just the way he used to when Deston was a boy.

Gradually, the image of Nigel faded, leaving Deston a very willing caretaker of Emmy's heart.

And when he glanced at the woman he loved before the doors closed, she beamed a smile at him, crooked teeth and all.

Little devil. He'd told her to save that strength a million times.

That night, at the small Wycliffe hospital, he stayed with her. Talked her to sleep with promises of always loving her the way she was. Of wanting more children.

Of taking care of the one that would survive all her lacerations and bruises.

He fell asleep by her side, holding her hand.

Dreaming of their future together.

Epilogue

On a sunny San Antonio morning, Emmy waited at the nursery doorway, watching her husband smile down at their one-month-old boy in his cradle.

He did it with such clear emotion that her heart swelled, bursting with love for both of them: Deston and the second Nigel.

A rainbow mobile danced slowly near Deston's head. When they'd moved to his luxury condo right after she'd gotten out of the hospital, he'd significantly cut back on office hours in order to be with his family. Now, he seemed contented, nowhere near as restless as the Deston she'd met last year.

As if he sensed her presence, he glanced up at her.

The power of his loving gaze almost pinned her to the condo floor. She crooked her finger at him and twiddled the sash of her silk robe, silently asking him to meet her in their room.

He did, of course, sweeping her into his arms, planting a passionate kiss on her mouth—one that sang through her veins and stretched them fully awake.

She ended it by rubbing her lips against his, smooching him, then burying her fingers in his thick brown hair. Hair the color of little Nigel's.

"It's too early to be up on the weekend," she said. "Even our boy isn't awake yet."

"I couldn't help peeking in on him." Deston slid his hands over her back—a whisper of skin on silk. "What're you doing up so early? I thought your mom was opening the restaurant?"

Francesca's. Deston had supported her in making this particular dream come true. Both Emmy and her mama had opened the River Walk eatery last week to rousing success. She was adamant about wanting to succeed on her own, to contribute to the family in her own way. Deston respected that, allowing her room to run the business.

He really was the perfect husband, she thought, biting her lip, pressing into his hard chest, rubbing silk against the cotton of his shirt.

"I'm up so early," she said, "because there was an empty space next to me in bed."

"Just appreciating the child I almost didn't have."

The memory of her car accident poked at Emmy. She'd been careless that day, blinded by sadness. When she thought of how she could've hurt her baby, her mama...

Deston was stroking the faint scar near her hairline. "I'm so damned lucky."

They all were. Even his family. It seemed that Emmy's entrance into her in-laws' lives had changed a few things around Oakvale, too. Rumor had it, said Felicia and Carlota, that the Mrs. was bunking with the Mr. again. And Deston had told her all about his father's business scheming and how he'd ended up doing right by Stanhope Steel in the end.

As Deston wrapped her in his arms, facing her forward and walking her toward a mirrored vanity table, Emmy grinned.

They'd even invited the real Lila Stanhope to the restaurant's opening. Emmy had been surprised to meet a demure woman who glowed with simple beauty—not the type to have a wham-bam affair, she imagined.

Then again, she'd never thought that of herself, either.

Deston had opened her jewelry box and taken out her locket. "If you're going to stop by the restaurant, let me help you get dressed. Let me serve *you,* ma'am."

He slipped the chain around her neck, and she stared at their image in the mirror.

A man holding a woman. A woman flushed with happiness and dreams come true.

"Know what's funny?" she asked. "For generations, my family has given all they've had to yours. And now I'm going to continue tradition and give you the most precious gift of all."

"A family." He nuzzled his lips against her neck.

"A big one."

She turned slightly, slid an arm around his neck, brushing her lips against his.

"Maybe instead of getting me dressed," she said, "we could turn the tables on expectation and…you know."

With a tug, he undid the sash of her robe. Smiled.

When she turned back to the mirror, he was leading the silk off her shoulder, baring it.

"Work can wait," he said, kissing his way down her skin.

The words escaped her as she treasured his kisses.

Her fantasy.

Her husband.

* * * * *

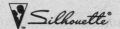

SPECIAL EDITION™

GOLD RUSH GROOMS
Lucky in love—and striking it rich—
beneath the big skies of Montana!

The excitement of Montana Mavericks: GOLD RUSH GROOMS continues

with

PRESCRIPTION: LOVE
(SE #1669)

by favorite author
Pamela Toth

City slicker Zoe Hart hated doing her residency in a one-horse town like Thunder Canyon. But each time she passed handsome E.R. doctor Christopher Taylor in the halls, her heart skipped a beat. And as they began to spend time together, the sexy physician became a temptation Zoe wasn't sure she wanted to give up. When faced with a tough professional choice, would Zoe opt to go back to city life—or stay in Thunder Canyon with the man who made her pulse race like no other?

Available at your favorite retail outlet.

Where love comes alive™

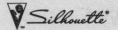

SPECIAL EDITION™

Introducing a brand-new miniseries by
Silhouette Special Edition favorite author
Marie Ferrarella

One special necklace,
three charm-filled romances!

BECAUSE A HUSBAND IS FOREVER

by Marie Ferrarella

Available March 2005
Silhouette Special Edition #1671

Dakota Delany had always wanted a marriage like
the one her parents had, but after she found her
fiancé cheating, she gave up on love. When her
radio talk show came up with the idea of having her
spend two weeks with hunky bodyguard Ian Russell,
she protested—until she discovered she wanted Ian
to continue guarding her body forever!

Available at your favorite retail outlet.

Where love comes alive™

Curl up and have a

Heart *to* Heart

with

Harlequin Romance®

Just like having a heart-to-heart
with your best friend, these stories
will take you from laughter to tears
and back again. So heartwarming
and emotional you'll want to
have some tissues handy!

Next month Harlequin is thrilled to bring you
Natasha Oakley's first book for Harlequin Romance:

For Our Children's Sake (#3838),
on sale March 2005

Then watch out for....

A Family For Keeps (#3843),
by Lucy Gordon, on sale May 2005

Available wherever Harlequin books are sold.

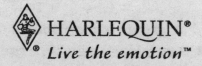